Published by

NIYOGI BOOKS

D-78, Okhla Industrial Area, Phase-I
New Delhi-110 020, INDIA
Tel: 91-11-26816301, 49327000
Fax: 91-11-26810483, 26813830
email: niyogibooks@gmail.com
website: www.niyogibooksindia.com

Editor: Gita Rajan
Layout Design: Ganga Kumar
Cover Design: Shashi Bhushan Prasad

ISBN: 978-93-85285-49-3
Publication: 2016

Printed at: Niyogi Offset Pvt. Ltd., New Delhi, India

'Karmanyewadhikaraste mafaleshu kadachana...'

(Bhagwad Gita)

To my step-mother

CONTENTS

In India

Whims, Twists and Drifts

THE warm autumn morning had begun with Laxmi arguing with her son Nawin. Nawin was six and had recently started school. Laxmi and Nawin were alone for a moment in the upper floor of the house where they lived. Her younger son Anil was with his father at the shop downstairs. Anil would join school the next year.

'The food you have given me has too much of salt and the curd is sour.'

'It cannot be,' Laxmi said. 'I have myself tasted the food.'

'No. It is not good,' Nawin insisted, sounding just like his father.

Laxmi already had a lot to do that morning, and had no time for Nawin's complaints. The real issue was he did not want to go to school, and she could do nothing about that.

She felt a little bitter. She had to go to the river to bring water. It was a walk to the steep stairs, then a long walk down those hard flat stone steps to the river. Then, as every morning, she would climb back with a pitcher full of water on her shoulder, after she had had a bath and done the laundry.

She never went there alone and instead accompanied the women of the neighbourhood. The women went around in a group when they went to a place like the riverbank (of the town called Ghat), which was secluded and reached after passing through a lonely stretch covered with trees on both sides. Drunken or deranged men lurked there, waiting to harass and harm unsuspecting victims.

Rapes too were common occurrences in case of women venturing out alone. But they were never reported, as it would only invite embarrassment.

Water was needed for cooking and cleaning, and it was a hardship to bring it from the river. Worst was the day when Laxmi had to haul water for everyone's bath. The children were never taken to the riverbank due to the fear of drowning. Dev was mostly busy at the shop to go to the river for a bath. Though he went there occasionally for a bath – on the day of the solar or lunar eclipse, or on days of similar religious significance.

Her husband and sons could have helped, but Dev thought it was solely Laxmi's job. Dev was twice her age, but was strong enough to carry water. He employed a labourer during Laxmi's monthly menstruation cycle to bring in the water. Because water touched by her was impure to drink or to cook with, during this period. Business at the shop was not bad, and they could have easily afforded paying for that service. Finding her husband indifferent to her hardship disappointed her, even though she tried to dutifully do her jobs. Her consolation was this near holiday of a week every month.

She was alarmed that her elder son was picking up his father's approach. So she reacted as she wanted to with her husband.

'If you argue with me like this I will go and drown myself in the river.'

Like his father, Nawin was angry and stubborn. 'I do not care.'

'You do not care if your mother dies?' she asked with irritation and exasperation.

'No, I don't.'

'Fine! I am going and will not return, ever!' With a great show she lifted the copper pitcher by its ring and stomped down the wooden stairs. When she was out of his sight, instead of walking out to the backyard, she hid under the stairs. Laxmi wanted to see what Nawin would do.

The boy tried to eat. But he felt his heart sink at the thought of his mother drowning in the river. It only took a couple of minutes before he ran down the stairs and out towards the river.

When he reached the top of the steep stairs, he looked down at the whole river bank. His mother was not among the women filling their pitchers, or among those washing clothes, or even those having a quick bath.

He saw a few men, a little distance away from the women, who were also either washing or having a bath. Nawin carefully looked at the people but his mother was nowhere in sight. Had she killed herself? Why had none of those people stopped her?

Tears forming, he walked slowly back to the house. Laxmi had seen everything, and now came from behind the stairs. She ran to Nawin and lifted him in her arms, kissing both of his cheeks, kissing away the tears while crying herself.

'So you do not care if your mother died?'

Nawin's reply was to push back and beat her chest with his tiny fists. 'Let me go!' He was angry. She played a game with him, and he had lost. Badly. Nawin hated that she had seen him crying for her.

Nawin had not expected his mother to tell his father about the matter. He thought she might have forgotten it during the day. Evening came. While they talked they also ate in the kitchen, next to the room they lived. Laxmi prepared and served hot rotis, directly from the wood fire.

Dev was particular about how dinner should be prepared and served. He told her regularly that a good cook should have three rotis in his or her hands. One on the *tawa* on the fire, another swelling in the fire; and a third one flattening on the *chowki*. 'Only then could one expect to feed all the family together,' he often said.

He practised what he insisted on every month for a week during which he had to cook, when Laxmi menstruated. Though washing was done by Laxmi during this period too, as the utensils dried in the sun after she washed them to become pure again for use. During this week she did not light the lamp near the idols of deities in the evenings. And the place remained dark.

Dev and the boys sat while she served the food. Then she joined them. They all sat on the floor on folded jute sacks. Dev sold grain too, along with other goods of daily necessity in the shop at the front of the house, and kept the empty sacks.

The family had many uses for the empty sacks. Some of the sacks that cushioned them still had their brightly coloured labels, announcing their emptied content and its weight, while the labels on others had faded to become unreadable.

When Laxmi told the story of the morning, a little excited and feeling vindicated, Dev looked at Nawin and smiled. Anil smiled also. She was a picture of youth among her very young children and middle-aged husband. She radiated a level of energy in her manners which often left them out of their breath.

After that incident Nawin was aware of his love for his mother. He knew he repressed showing it because that was what his father did. Now it had come out. He expected his mother to refrain from telling about it to his brother and father. But she betrayed him, and now he felt more infuriated than ever.

IT was sometime during the winter when there were elections. It was the first for Nawin and he was fascinated by the spectacle.

A jeep came to Ghat one day with several small colourful flags tied to it. While it moved the flags unfurled like the movement of a serpent. They dropped when it stopped. Those rectangular flags had a symbol of a cow feeding a calf. The campaigners forbade the children who tried to snatch away the flags. Speeches were made by people sitting in the jeep between the filmy songs, through two loudspeakers attached to its roof facing opposite directions, and pamphlets were distributed. The loudspeakers, in between, also belted out slogans like:

Jansangh ko vote do,
Bidi pina chod do,
Bidi mein tambaku hai,
Congress wala daku hai.
(Vote for Jansangh, quit smoking bidi contains tobacco,
Congress is a party of dacoits.)

This catchy slogan was picked up by the children of the town. They shouted it, making it into a chorus, for many days after the jeep left. Before the campaigners left, they gave the children the coveted flags, and the children ran around the main street of the town with the flags in their hands, chanting the slogan.

When the results came in, some people were pleased that Indira Gandhi's Congress party had won the elections. They expressed the hope that, being the daughter of Nehru, she would lead the people and the country in the right direction. By then, many grown up girls already bore the name Indira.

People unfailingly listened to the quarter-to-nine evening news on All India Radio, in Hindi. It reported the exciting things that were happening across the country. Few people actually had radios during those days as it needed a government license to have one, which needed to be renewed every year at the post office.

After receiving fifteen rupees the post office clerk put the ticket on the radio license books and stamped them. One could buy a decent pair of leather shoes with that money at that time. Government officials - who looked as if they belong to another species and not the human one - came routinely looking for radios with non-renewed licenses, to extract bribes.

A shop selling paan, which had a radio, was the most sought-after meeting place during the evening news hour except during winter. People went there after dinner to hear the news. During summers, the homes were too hot to remain inside till midnight.

The radio would be switched on at full volume. People listened to it while chewing paan, with tobacco or without. Some tried to talk, spitting the red, paan-laced saliva collected in their mouth, when the news confirmed or denied something, that piqued or intrigued them. More people tried to join the ensuing debate. Someone who was listening to the news most attentively would inevitably ask them to stop talking.

Towards the end, by the time it was the turn for news on sports, which the youngsters listened to attentively, the elders would have left.

The volume of the radio came down when the news in English followed the Hindi version, which almost no one among those present understood. Then the frequency was changed to the station playing movie songs, like Radio Ceylon.

The evenings were not lit by electricity, as it had not reached the town yet. The shops still open at that hour were lit by hissing petromax lights: the lights had a glowing bulb of cotton threads, into which fuel was pumped in a very thin stream; indeed. If dirt in the fuel obstructed the stream, a pin was needed to clear it. Those petromaxes, so often used in the town almost every evening in every shop, were only used either in a marriage or a religious ceremony, in a neighbouring village. In that village, only a handful of people knew how to operate a petromax. So once its stream of fuel was to be cleared by a pin, it became a crisis if someone knowledgeable was not around.

NAWIN'S father took them out of town very often.

At times they went to a bigger town, Sora, by bus, to draw his pension.

Dev was a retired soldier who had quit the armed services before the age of forty. He was recruited when the World War was at its peak and Mahatma Gandhi had called for the Quit India movement. He was a Nepali citizen during a time when the currency of India and Nepal was considered equal and silver coins with the impression of Queen Victoria were in circulation. There was always a shortage of recruits in the army as the war was taking a very high toll after it had spread the world over. It was not considered that he was a citizen of Nepal and his village was mentioned under Almora district, instead of Baitadi. He was one of the sepoys deployed in Burma by the British-Indian government. But by then the war was inching towards its end. He did not see much action, though he had been sent to a war front.

He had a chance, however, to see the Japanese and the German Prisoners-of-War during those years. He remembered the German POWs defeating the British Indian army by more than a dozen goals in a trial football match. The skilled Japanese POWs made a cigarette case out of emptied food cans overnight. It had a button. When it was pressed, out came a cigarette! The POWs sold these cases to sepoys like Dev serving in the British army.

Dev told Nawin that earlier roads had not been constructed in that area and he had to walk for three days to reach the nearest railway station whenever he came home on leave or returned to his military duty. But after Indian independence road construction took place in those hills and the need to walk on foot gradually reduced. When he retired from his job in 1961, he had to still walk for a day to reach home. He was given an exemplary ranking in his discharge certificate, which he found pride in, as he didn't grow up much in ranks.

He thought his gain was the observation of life of various people and places he came in contact with during his service years. One of the big setbacks of the service years was he had no children alive. His wife, who he married when he had just entered his teens, and she had not attained puberty gave birth a few times but the new-borns couldn't survive. Either they were stillborn or an epidemic took them away. She was probably too much burdened by domestic duties to take care of the babies. Dev felt sadder, whenever he got the news of the death of yet another daughter or son of his. He became desperate to quit his job and begin a family when he reached his thirties. He took retirement at the first available opportunity.

Finding that his wife was not able to bear him children anymore, he married for the second time. Fortunately, with Laxmi, his second wife, he had two sons within a few years of their marriage. He left his village Dhura to build a life on the Indian side of the border, where a business town was emerging very fast. He started with a small grocery shop and it took off briskly. He built a house in the town which was a decent looking three storey building. Birth of two sons from a young second wife rekindled his hopes of a better life.

They went to their native-village, Dhura, often, in the other country across the river, climbing the hills for three hours, to offer prayers at the temple there.

Nawin did not yet have the eye to see the embarrassment his mother felt on going out with her husband, who was shorter than her and twice her age.

Although she acted normal, occasionally she was different. He once heard her telling his father that a few young men of the town had tried to accost her when she went out alone. She liked it when at Dhura the younger cousins of her husband paid attention to her or plied her with compliments. With them and their wives, her manner was domineering, as she was the wife of a man with cash, property and a successful business in town.

Cash was as scarce as ever in the villages. It was pulled to the town in one way or another, leaving the villagers in perpetual destitution. But unless they were seriously sick, the villagers were self-sufficient. They grew their food and had a house to live.

Once Laxmi went to visit her parents, taking Anil with her. It was several hours' walk further from Dhura into the hills, to reach her parents. She returned only after a month. During this time his father did the cooking and washing for both Nawin and himself, although he employed labourers to fetch water from the river.

When Laxmi and Anil returned, they brought with them a goat. It was only a few weeks old, and milky-white in colour. Nawin soon grew fond of it. He took the kid in his lap while he roamed the streets of the town. He fed it and talked to it for hours, caressing its soft white fur. It looked beautiful with its big black eyes and pink-coloured eyelids.

A few weeks later horns appeared on its head. One morning his parents took away the kid, saying that they were going to the temple in the town. When they returned the kid was not with them. When Nawin asked about it, they gave him evasive answers. Only that evening, when they served him dinner, was Nawin told that the meat he was about to eat was that of the goat. They had slaughtered it to offer a sacrifice at the temple.

He fell silent, and did not eat that evening. For several months afterwards, he did not eat meat, as the sight of it reminded him of that kid. Eventually, however, Nawin became accustomed to the ritual of animal-sacrifice. It was routinely performed at the temple on a religious occasion in the town or at Dhura.

Their village temple was a short climb away in the hills further from Dhura. It was in the middle of a pine-forest. No one lived there, so it had a mysterious appearance. The villagers however, came there often, to offer prayers, even when it was not a religious occasion. Living by the lunar calendar, everyday was important for the people. It was the calendar which mostly defined the routine and rituals of the people. If taken away, people might have been at a loss to organise their lives.

Some days were particularly auspicious to ritually offer prayers with animal sacrifice at the temple. At times more than a dozen goats were sacrificed on a day and every villager attended the ceremony.

But there were also ordinary days when villagers casually visited the temple alone. A death or a birth among the families of the villagers rendered them impure to enter inside the boundary of the temple, even when the days were the most auspicious.

The religious occasions often began in the evening and continued late into the night. Inside, the temple was poorly lit by candles, where the priest of the village offered prayers. Outside, there was light from the fires in the open, around which children played and some elders talked. In the wilderness of the forest, at night, the fires gave a ghostly appearance. At the end of the ceremony the animals were slaughtered inside the temple.

Their corpses were roasted on the fires outside, fed continuously with pine wood or cones. Some of the pine cones or wood were lying on the ground, but most were in the trees. The young village boys climbed the pine trees effortlessly to get them. Nawin could not do that, for he was a boy grown-up in a town, where there was hardly ever a need to climb a tree. He marvelled at such skills, which were absent in town-boys like him.

Thin, dried stems of pine were used to remove the burnt hair from the skin of the goat, by scratching. During this process the meat was already half-cooked. The skin broke, making the hot juices ooze out with a sizzling sound.

Nawin saw the children of the village snatching away a burnt tail or the oozing-out meat with their hands, and eating it without letting it cool. They were probably hungry and impatient, waiting too long into the night till the goats were ritually sacrificed and roasted in their skins. He remained ambivalent about meat-eating, however, often dropping it to eventually take it up again.

NAWIN was reluctant to get up. The night had been too hot for a sound sleep. But it was a cool morning. His father was trying to persuade him to get out of bed and have tea with a roti, before going to school.

During summer months, school was over by mid-day. In between there was a 'half-time', at around 9:00 am, for half an hour. During it, he and Anil, who had started to go to school last winter, returned home running, to have the breakfast prepared by Laxmi. Then they hastily ran back to school, where the monitor beat a brass plate with a wooden hammer. The bell divided time into different periods at the school.

That day he was walking back to the school after half-time, leaving Anil still eating. Laxmi had served them hot kheer. Nawin left after she went with a pitcher to get water from the river while they were still eating, warning them before she left to finish their food before they returned to school, or they would be punished when they returned from the school.

On the way to school, Nawin heard people talking about a woman who had been rescued from drowning in the river by a swimmer. The swimmer caught her at a broad space downstream, where the fast current of the river was slowed down by large rocks. The water whirled and circled before it flowed into a narrow passage under the bridge with a furious speed. This movement of water between the rocks created a steady sound heard in the town, a sound that was a witness and background to everything happening in it, filling the moments of silence as well.

Nawin heard people say that the woman rescued was breathing her last. He slowed as he saw his neighbour running towards the hospital, which was at the end of the town near his school. The neighbour looked ridiculous in his kurta, pyjama and a boat-shaped cap of coarse-cotton.

Nawin smiled at him and tried to run along with him.

'Run Nawin run,' he said, 'or you will be late for the school.'

His lips tight, sweat was running down his face on a morning getting increasingly hotter. He looked at Nawin with affection, but he also looked very worried. They parted when Nawin turned towards his school and the neighbour to the hospital. Nawin slowed to catch his breath.

A friend came up. 'Have you heard anything?'

'Yes. I heard that a woman has been rescued from drowning by an expert swimmer. And she is in a serious condition.'

'You don't know?' They both stopped. 'It is your mother.'

Nawin was stunned. Speechless. Tears blinded his vision.

He returned home running faster than he ever had. He found his father at the shop, lying on the bench in front of it, in grief. Neighbouring shop-keepers were trying to console him.

It turned out the neighbour Nawin had met was running to get a doctor. Laxmi was on the bank of the river, dead. The wife of another neighbour called Nawin to her home. There he found Anil, crying silently. He held a banana in his hands but was not eating.

The other women of the neighbourhood had gathered there. They were sympathetically touching the faces of both brothers, wiping away their tears. One woman told another that though their mother had died, the golden jewellery she wore had been recovered, along with her body. They told the boys that that was good. Because sometimes people simply disappeared in the river. It was no consolation for Nawin and Anil.

A stoic silence enveloped the boys. Their father did not come to find them. He was busy cremating his wife on that hot afternoon, with the help of his neighbours and friends in the town. He returned in the evening, tired and grieving. He looked at Nawin and Anil with pity but said nothing. None of them ate the food which was provided by their neighbour. They sat in silence.

The river had an unpredictable flow during summer as the heat melted fast the snow which fed the river. Its water was freezing cold to touch when it reached that hot town on its bank many miles downstream. People drank it to cool themselves before it got hotter. It was probably a gush of water which drowned Laxmi, who was taking her bath, as was informed by the neighbour who accompanied her.

The next few days were days of mourning. But the mourning was to continue for Nawin and Anil for the rest of their lives.

Their father grieved for his young wife while relations visited and discussed in whispers what would happen to the two motherless boys. One day, Nisha, his father's first wife, arrived. She lived with her parents after Dev had taken a second wife.

Nawin met her when someone asked him to show her the cow and the calf they kept in a shed in the backyard. While he was about to return, after showing her the place, Nisha touched his chin with her palm and wept for a while, without saying anything. He felt overwhelmed by this gesture.

She started cooking and washing for them.

On the thirteenth day of mourning, Nawin, Anil and their father went to a big Peepal tree in the outskirts of the town to offer final prayers for the peaceful resting of the soul of Laxmi.

Nawin noticed, among other rituals, a gold coin was wrapped in a white cotton cloth, and tied around the tree. Then prayers were offered by the priest and his father. The priest took the coin at the end, apart from the other offerings made in the ceremony.

The days of summer seemed endless, with the bright sunlight illuminating everything so starkly that the future looked distant. Nawin and Anil had grown very sensitive to the sympathy expressed. They wanted to mourn their loss in private. Life however, had become full of events and crowded by people who came to express condolences to their father.

A few days later, one of Laxmi's sisters arrived with her brothers. Nawin heard that she would be the next wife of his father. He was startled. His heart had already been won by Nisha, who so affectionately touched his chin that day in the cow-shed and wept, but had said nothing.

Also, their neighbour's wife, who gave them food before Nisha arrived, prompted him to object to his father taking another young wife, even though she was a sister of his mother. She said out of this marriage there could be more children in the family and this would make things worse for Nawin and his brother. Besides the woman was too young to marry his father. It convinced Nawin.

For Nawin, the stakes were as high as they could be. He decided to confront his father. He declared that he would accept no one in his mother's place but Nisha, or he would leave the home.

A few days later Laxmi's sister and the others left, and Nisha's place was established in their lives.

DURING the next few months it looked as if matters had settled down a little and life had returned to a routine. Nawin and Anil started to go to school, again. The memory of their mother was always there in their hearts. Her image of warning them to finish the food was the last one they had, as no one remembered to show them her body before it was cremated. It was a tragedy that seemed to have shocked and overwhelmed most of the people they knew, to the extent that they forgot the young boys, who had become motherless.

The brothers did not discuss this matter, and fell silent if a visitor mentioned their mother's early death and pitied them. Nawin went away on such occasions. Anil was too young. His loss must have been greater than his own - Nawin often thought.

But soon there was another surprise in store. Within a year, Nisha became pregnant and delivered a boy. He was very frail and weak.

On the ninth day of his birth he was named Dinesh after a proper religious ceremony. Young girls of the neighbourhood came to Dev to ask for some money as gift to them on the birth of a son. Nawin saw his father doling out a few coins from his shirt pocket looking embarrassed.

It looked as if Dinesh would not survive his first few years as he was not capable to walk even after two years and made only a few unintelligible sounds. He was often sick and suffered constipation and fever. But slowly he improved and started walking due to the efforts of Nisha and Dev. Then he began running in the streets making loud unclear noises.

However he was not normal. Both Dev, into his fifties now, and Nisha, in her forties, massaged him with oil whenever they were free.

However, as the doctor too confirmed, he was mentally challenged, with very little chances of recovery. His parents did not accept this fact easily. Dev kept on trying to make him learn the alphabets and numbers in the following years. His efforts worked, though slowly.

It was a time-taking and arduous work. Dinesh claimed all the attention of Dev and Nisha and Nawin felt that he and Anil were not getting proper attention. Somehow they continued with their studies and went to a higher class with good marks every year.

NAWIN won a scholarship to join high school in a bigger town. Almora, a day's drive away from his home, high in the hills, was much further from Sora. Dev, however, wanted him to stay back and continue his studies at the school in their town, where, by now, the classes for high school too had started to run. Nawin was adamant – he wanted to leave. Just thirteen-years-old, he thought of living independently. He was not happy with the crowded life he had at home.

As once before with his father, Nawin again won the battle of wills. For his admission at the new school, Dev came along with him. They reached Almora after a drive of a full day in a rickety bus which broke down twice. They stayed at a hotel that evening.

The journey took them climbing many towering mountains and descending into the valleys, crossing many rivers, at times entering into the shallow rivers which had no bridges. Every turn in the road opened a new picturesque view of many layers of mountains before the mighty Himalayas. There were valleys deep down, with houses between the green crops in the fields.

Nawin was fascinated by the journey. He had never travelled such a long distance before in a bus. Dev explained how often he had travelled this distance on foot, when he was in the army. He told that there were mules and horses to hire, to carry one's luggage. Many of the people running those mules and horses had settled after the roads were constructed to build a business in the towns near the road.

Dev told Nawin that a few of them, who were of Nepali nationality, had migrated to Kathmandu and had established themselves in a business or a job there. He often reminded Nawin that his future probably would be more secure in Nepal than in India. But Nawin ignored such talks.

Thrilled and also tired, he slept soundly in the hotel. But Dev was worried, and he did not sleep well. He was concerned about what would happen the next day, and after he would leave behind Nawin at the hostel.

Next day, Nawin was admitted to the class and the hostel. It was a cloudy day and it rained intermittently. Nawin asked his father to buy him a plastic hat to save him from rain. With the hat on, he attracted queer glances of the students when he waited with his father to see the Principal. His father asked him to remove it when they entered the Principal's room.

The principal was a tall and fair man with a kind heart and pleasant manners. He introduced them to the warden of the hostel sitting in the room and listened to Dev carefully. He assured Dev that they would take proper care of Nawin after Dev left him at the hostel.

Nawin felt a little intimidated by the formal way they talked to his father. He was not sure what would happen after his father left him alone. He was asked to attend the remaining classes running during the day. His father encouraged him to go to the class while he waited at the school gates. Nawin found the class but couldn't concentrate on the lessons.

The hostel warden welcomed them when they reached the hostel after the classes. He showed them the room where Nawin had to stay with two more scholarship students who were yet to arrive. There was a cot, a bookshelf and table and chair set for each of them.

Dev thanked the warden and asked if he could stay that night at the hostel. The warden allowed it as a special case.

Dev started opening the holdall which contained Nawin's mattress. Then he opened the bags that contained their towels and other clothes. He told Nawin that he would leave enough money with him to buy his books and stationery. He reminded Nawin that he will be getting the scholarship money every month from the school, from which he will have to pay for the food and other things. Dev added that whatever more money Nawin would need he would arrange to send it through the drivers who drove the bus between their town and Almora every alternate day.

The hostel canteen was a little distance away, where two meals and two teas were served every day. They both went there to eat. It was crowded with senior students. The food was very different from what Nawin was used to. He disliked it and became gloomy. Looking at him Dev too became sad. He was not sure if Nawin was ready for life away from home.

On the following morning, Dev got up early to catch the bus home. Nawin went with him to the bus stop to see him off.

Nawin suddenly panicked when the bus was about to leave, at the thought of living alone at a place so far away from home. The school building had a very high ceiling above the mighty walls, which began to appear strange to him. The furniture and teachers in the class began to crowd his mind, everything so unfamiliar.

Also Almora was much bigger and the roads were crowded than Ghat or Sora. He started to cry, finding that his father was about to leave him alone.

His father became grim and he too shed tears on seeing Nawin cry. Dev never forgot that he was far too old to be Nawin's father. In fact, many of his contemporaries had a grandson Nawin's age. He had lost hope of having children when he was young. He also felt pity for Nawin and Anil for they had lost their mother so early in their lives.

He urged Nawin once again to drop the idea of staying away from his family, as he was very young. In their confusion and tears, which had attracted the attention of other passengers, as the bus was getting late on their account, Dev got down from the bus with his luggage and let it leave. They both returned to the hostel. The hostel warden was surprised when Dev explained. He was a kind man though. When he became aware of the early death of Nawin's mother he became sympathetic. He urged Dev to take his time and take a proper decision. For it was a matter of Nawin's education and career.

Along with Nawin, another boy named Shyam had also come from a small town like his, who also had won the scholarship. Shyam had been admitted to the school and the hostel on the same day. To Shyam's father, who accompanied his son like Dev, Dev explained the whole matter. Shyam's father was surprised that Dev was ready to cancel the admission and take Nawin back home.

He took Nawin and Dev, along with his son Shyam, to a restaurant that evening, and while they were having snacks and tea, he advised Nawin to stick to his earlier decision of living independently.

'After all you will have to do it at some stage,' he said, 'and you will not be alone at the hostel, as many other boys on the scholarship will join you along with my own son, Shyam. By returning home now you will be missing the chance of being educated at one of the most reputed schools of the area.'

His persuasions worked, and Nawin decided to stay. The sternness he did not find in his father, to over-rule him, he found in the father of another boy. Shyam was to remain his close friend for the next few years that they stayed at that school and hostel.

Now Nawin came home only on holidays. Anil continued to attend the school in their home town. Every time he came home, Nawin found his father and Nisha busy trying to improve the learning capacity of Dinesh. Anil looked lost and lonely amidst them as Dinesh consumed all the time and attention of his parents.

By the time he was ten, Dinesh was able to read a few lines and write his name. Efforts to make him learn calculations proved futile, however. Dev also trained Dinesh on how to use the toilet and then clean himself, and how to brush his teeth. Raising Dinesh was a job requiring a lot of patience, to which Dev and Nisha were fully dedicated.

Nawin was old enough to think about his future. He noticed that preoccupation with Dinesh had made Dev lose interest in the business. He was taking loans to meet the expenses of the household and that of his education. If things didn't change the future could prove bleak for all of them. But Dev was too preoccupied with Dinesh to look at these things. Nawin worried about his future and that of Anil.

Once a certificate of his nationality was required for Nawin to appear in the entrance test to a medical school, when he was in the final year at school. Dev tried his best but couldn't obtain it. The official told him that though Dev and his family were living in India and owned a property there, their ancestors were Nepalis. It disheartened Nawin a great deal. He remembered his father often advising him to seek a job and career in Nepal. But he had never seen Nepal beyond his occasional visit to Dhura.

The circumstances were making him feel adrift with nothing solid to cling too. The burden of loans took a toll on Dev's health. He had developed a cardiac problem and was not capable of working anymore. But more money was needed to pay for Nawin's education as he was about to enter college. Soon Anil would follow him. Without a college education, the chances of making a proper living were very little for Nawin and Anil.

The kind neighbour, who Nawin had seen running to fetch a doctor to attend to his dying mother, often took interest in what Nawin did. He advised him repeatedly to do well in his studies. He reminded him of the great hardship his father faced arranging money for Nawin and depended on him a great deal due to his old age and sickness.

But Nawin was uncertain of the future. The life he had seen so far was proving unreal as he didn't belong legally to the society and the people and the country he thought as his own.

He was worried how he could build a life from scratch in a country he had not really seen and amongst people he had never met. The responsibilities on him were immense. His father consoled him with assurances that he had a few connections in Kathmandu, when he went there to try his luck to find a job.

Kathmandu was a place full of mystery and romance to Nawin. Without having ever seen it, he felt if his fate was tied to it by destiny. Kathmandu was a much fabled name to which a great lure was attached. It was nothing familiar like Delhi or Bombay, where so many of the people Nawin knew lived and worked. There was never a clue about how life would be in Kathmandu.

Nepal

National Games and Job Scenarios

FINDING no jobs at hand after his graduation, Nawin decided to go to Nepal. His father encouraged him to do so. By now there was an urgency that he found a job and reduced his father's burden.

For a while, he stayed in Dhangadi, a town on the way to Kathmandu. His cousins ran a chemist's shop there and he helped at the shop in the mornings.

The third Nepalese National Games were about to take place in Birganj. The youngest brother of the king, Prince Dhirendra, was the Chairman of the Organising Committee. There were district and zonal level sub-committees to select the players. They extorted money from almost every businessman and more especially taxed the goods coming from India, at the customs office on the border. They stopped every vehicle passing through a highway, except the government ones, and extracted money in the name of National Games.

The preparations for the National Games appeared to be the main activity taking place in the town and around it, mobilising many people and touching the life of even more. The selected players in different sports were offered free food and sports kits.

The games were even more political than they appeared. It was an effort to consolidate the existing system from the grass-root level by selecting young men as players and then indoctrinating them with the philosophy of the establishment: that the country was because of the king and not the other way.

Players were fed at a restaurant called Moti Mahal, in Dhangadi, run by a Sikh from India. He often complained that the players ate heartily at his hotel, for which he was paid a fixed amount – a very nominal one. 'Moti Mahal will go bankrupt, if the games do not take place soon,' he lamented frequently.

Nawin, while at college, was selected to play Badminton for his university. He decided to take part in the Nepalese National Games. He was a new face in town, so he was told he was not eligible for free-food. He paid for his meals at Moti Mahal, but got a chance to practise for free. It was a break for him from his time at the shop.

One day the Secretary of the National Sports Council, Binod Shah, came to Dhangadi. He was barely four-feet and had the face of a monkey. Two beautiful girls (purportedly reporters) were besides him on either side, towering over him while he accepted the salutes of the sportsmen gathered there to welcome him on the grounds near the sports-office and the badminton hall.

He had come to take stock of how the preparations for the games were taking place in Dhangadi.

Behind the Badminton hall was a much bigger ground, which, Nawin came to know, had earlier served as an air-strip. In fact, it was very difficult to run round it, even once, even for the best of the training athletes. No one ever practised there. The smaller ground on the east of the hall was popular amongst the sportsmen, as it had running tracks made of red clay, outlined by white lime-powder. These markings had to be refreshed every week, as they blew away while the athletes practised.

The old air-strip was uneven, apart from being too big to practise. It was almost abandoned like any other flat land, in the great expanse of Dhangadi. It amused Nawin to think that just next to the town landed small aircrafts, when the air-strip was in operation. Back, then, people walked out of their flights directly into town to catch a rickshaw to reach their destination.

Recently, the airport had shifted about ten miles away from the town, in the north, between dense forests which surrounded it on three sides. Flights were infrequent; around once a week. People disembarking had to walk for half a mile from the airport to reach an unpaved road. Only from there could one catch a bus. However, when senior government officials landed, an official-jeep waited at the air-strip to pick them up. They would give a lift to the other passengers, if the officials permitted.

Dhangadi had a reputation of being a town to which the civil servants were transferred as a punishment. It was inaccessible by road from other major towns of the country on the one hand, while flying to it was no pleasure either, on the other.

However, the forests surrounding the new air-strip were being cleared very fast, by the people descending from the hills in ever-increasing numbers and settling in the huts made of wood and mud. There was a possibility that Dhangadi too would spread out as a major emerging town, a few years down the line. And then the story of the old air-strip would disappear from the memory, after it became covered by concrete buildings, constructed by the people who had already started encroaching on it.

Binod Shah gave a speech and sang the song of the forthcoming National Games, before the national anthem. He was a powerful man and was considered amongst the closest to the royal family. He was seen to be on his knees with both his hands joined when in the presence of the King – just like Hanuman in the presence of Lord Rama, in a religious poster.

This tyranny Binod Shah perpetuated on the people under him, expecting the same submissiveness from them. But most of the sportsmen, if not the officials, ridiculed him after he left a day later, speculating on how he would have made love to one of the reporters, or to both of them, during the night he stayed in Dhangadi. They laughed most at his short stature and monkey-face.

However, despite his physical limitations he had successfully managed to acquire immense power, through the patronage of the royals.

He was indoctrinating and regimenting the most able-bodied youth to support and favour the king's regime and tyranny, right from the grass-root level across the country, while he organised the National Games. As it involved the accumulation and spending of a large amount of money, it was assumed that he was making a fortune for himself as well in the bargain.

Nawin managed to defeat the other players of the town, after he trained and practised more. He became the leading badminton player of Dhangadi. But the coach wasn't happy.

He had seen the players in other parts of the country. He knew that they were far better than the players he had with him. He wanted them to train more.

He found that they were talented but were deficient technically. Their steps were haphazard. He tried to explain it to them. However, most of the young men were interested only in the outing they might have through the National Games. Others were around mainly as they had young women players around during the practice sessions. Nawin too was unsure about his future as a player. No one he knew had made a career in it. It was at best a hobby for someone with a regular job or a business.

Recently, an Indian player, Prakash Padukonė, had won the All England championship of Badminton. It invited the interest of many young players. But a career in sports was too much hard work with rewards only for a champion. Besides it was not inexpensive to practise as a professional player.

The winter was at its fag end and the date of the National Games was approaching very fast.

They started for Birganj on a spring day, on three dilapidated buses run by some Sikh-businessmen from India. The riots after the assassination of Indira Gandhi had pushed many Sikh families into Nepal. Industrious as they were, they had briskly established themselves in different businesses. The buses had to pass through the Indian Territory as Dhangadi was not yet connected to Nepalgunj by roads then. The buses broke down often and only by 10:00 pm did they reach Nepalgunj. Nepalgunj was the other important town on the way to Birgunj.

A hotel, still open, was asked to cook food for nearly two hundred players and officials, who were very hungry by then. And it took time. Only by early morning were Nawin and all the other people fed.

They then drove for another day and night to reach Birgunj. In between they took a long break at Butwal, where the buses received major repairs, taking several hours.

There were little arrangements to accommodate them and the other players arriving from all over the country, they discovered on their arrival. They were lodged in a school, and were expected to rest or sleep on the floor of the class-rooms. The furniture had been removed and beds were prepared of dried grass, covered by a jute sheet. The athletes rested after a tiring journey. Some of them opted for the veranda, as it had fresh air. In the canteen of the school food was served. Which Nawin found to be fresh and sumptuous.

There were only a few toilets and a single hand-pump in the open, to draw water for washing purposes. The players had started to go behind the bushes to relieve themselves, next to the fields, in-front of the school courtyard, where the crops were growing. They found that the latrines were over-crowded and it was impossible to wait in the long queues. Women players, however, about twenty in number, negotiated with a residential house in the neighbourhood to use its toilet and hand-pump to wash – which were otherwise meant for the servants of the house. It saved them the ignominy of waiting in a queue along with the men outside the latrine, or going to bushes next to them; or washing from a common hand-pump, while the men ogled at their bodies.

Mosquitoes attacked in droves and the nets to avoid them were limited in supply. So, often, two people shared a mosquito-net while sleeping on a bed on the floor. Thankfully, it was early spring, and the mornings were still a little cold. In the heat of summer such living conditions might have made many of them ill, in spite of the good physical condition they were in.

The women players took part in various sports, including the Dohari Geet, a competition of singing folk songs. In this game, the players had to improvise the lyrics in reply to other lyrics, and sing them to the beat of a *madal*. The other lyrics were questions improvised and sung by the competing team from another zone. Their musical practice sessions attracted all the players of the group to crowd into their room, and added some charm to the otherwise gloomy atmosphere among the players about the poor housing arrangements. It was also time for the young men and women to have some fun on the side. They were away from their families and there were no restrictions on their intermingling. By the evening many of them had gone to see the town of Birgunj in pairs. Nawin found the circumstances too stultifying to think of anything romantic or intimate.

Food served was not bad though, it was proved again and again by the speed with which it disappeared amongst the athletes looking for more. Hundreds of eggs were boiled in a large pot and they were served very hot to the players who competed to get them from across the counter. Similar was the fate of the jam toast served.

Inauguration of the Games was to take place the next morning. The king was expected to come from Kathmandu.

Everybody got up early to have breakfast and reach the stadium by bus, by six in the morning, attired in the T-shirt and half pants and the black *Bhadgaunle topi* provided by the organisers. On the back of the T-shirt the name of the zone the players and officials represented was mentioned. An identity card hung from their necks. Different zones were given a dress of different colour. So when the inaugural ceremony actually took place the colourful mélange the dresses of players created in the parade was a charming sight.

Falling in line with other players of his zone after they reached the stadium, Nawin too waited for the arrival of the king. The morning chill was gone, and the temperature grew by the hour.

It was midday when the king finally landed near the stadium in a military helicopter. By that time Nawin and other participants felt harassed as the heat had grown steadily. The players from all fourteen zones of the country were paraded into the stadium on the running tracks. Loudspeakers announced their zones and the special features of the zones, such as the rivers and mountains, and the festivals and the people. At each announcement, the crowd cheered. The stadium by now had filled in full to capacity.

The athletes saluted the king and the queen, who were sitting on a raised pavilion in the stadium, the only portion of the stadium with a roof, as they passed by the royal couple. After saluting they fell into neat lines in the middle of the field, facing the royal couple.

Then officials seated near the king started their speeches.

The speeches (the longest one by Binod Shah), all concluded by loudly hailing the king and the queen. The loudspeakers, which were already making a low-screeching sound, due to some technical problem, reduced the speeches to noise. The hailing of the king and the queen were the loudest and the most audible part of any speech above the screeching.

Most of the audience and the players repeated the hailing thankfully, for it also meant that one more speech was over. Nawin could see the restive faces of the players around him, apart from a few who had reverence written on them, and they were mostly feminine.

The king finally declared the Games open, wishing the players success. Nawin expected him to say a little more, but he did not. He noticed the queen scanning the surroundings with her binoculars. The youngest brother of the king, Prince Dhirendra, was sitting near him. He was the patron of the National Sports Council.

Then the royal couple left in the helicopter they had arrived in, which once again raised a lot of dust that filled the stadium when it took off. The inauguration ceremony was over, as the dust settled down.

Before they returned to the school building they were staying in, Nawin was told that his match was scheduled for that evening, in a hall near a small pond only a walking distance away. Physically tired and mentally harassed, he requested it to be postponed, as he needed some rest and practice.

But the officials declared it was not possible. He lost the game in straight sets and the National Games for him were over. As it was for his team; the other players too had put in equally poor performances. They could only win a doubles game, losing all four singles. He thought at least he could rest now, but he was told that the next morning he would have to leave, along with the other players losing in the opening rounds of different games. He resisted, saying that he was too unwell to take that gruelling two days' journey back. One of the officials relented and allowed him to stay – until the second bus left, the next day.

It was a pleasant surprise that the weight-lifters of his zone won a few medals that evening and the next. Also the football team of women from his zone made it to the semi-finals later.

Having time to himself now, the next morning Nawin took the rounds of the Birgunj bazaar and bought a bottle of Chinese hair shampoo and a shirt. The shopkeepers he talked to lamented that big money was extorted from them by the officials organising the Games promising them big business in return. But very few of the athletes did any purchasing so far, they complained.

That evening Prince Dhirendra came to visit the place they were staying. They were asked to stand in line on both the sides of their room or veranda, next to their beds on the floor, bowing their heads so as to not meet his eyes, and clap as he passed by.

They were allowed to look at his back once he had passed.

However, no one mentioned what to do when he returned after finishing his inspection. While he returned, the Prince found everybody staring at him. Prince Dhirendra mostly wore black glasses while in public, so his face was expressionless. He was a handsome man of short height.

Nawin had seen him earlier that day while he was walking on a road near the bazaar. The prince was driving a SUV by himself. He looked in askance at Nawin and smiled when Nawin recognised him and wished him while he went past.

It was speculated by the players after he left that he had come looking for a girl who would sleep with him that night. He had a bad reputation. Once while Prince Dhirendra was in Pokhra, a tourist town to the west of Kathmandu, the bodies of two young girls were found on the banks of River Seti, on a morning. They were raped before being killed. It was the prince behind the crime, people suspected, since he was in town. However, no one was ever apprehended or tried for the crime. The people who accompanied him on such an excursion outside Kathmandu had a criminal reputation.

Seti river disappears between the rocks on which Pokhra town is situated, as soon it enters the town. It flows underneath making a loud roaring noise while its water churns between the narrow arrangements of rocks. The river appears again at the foothills of Pokhra in the south, as calm and noiseless as it was before it entered the town. The disappearance of Seti river under the town and the sound of it flowing under it gave Pokhra a mysterious touch.

However, the immense Fewa lake, nearly seven kilometres long, and the Begnas lake, a little distance away from Pokhra town, made it a town of immense natural beauty. On a clear day, the mighty Fishtail Himalayan peak and other snow-covered peaks of Annapurna mountain range are reflected in the waters of the lakes, presenting a fascinating sight. The tourists crowded Pokhra in incredible numbers, to savour its natural beauty. The sensational double murder of two young, good-looking girls there, while Prince Dhirendra and his cohorts were in town was fresh in the memories of the people. It became a topic of discussion in low voices amongst them, whenever Prince Dhirendra was around.

Next evening, Nawin and other losing players in different games were dispatched back to Dhangadi, on the second bus. Its Sikh driver-owner was complaining during the whole trip that he was paid far less than he was promised by the organisers of the National Games.

NAWIN lingered for a while in Dhangadi, after the Games. Further college education appeared pointless. The National Games was a distraction at best, from the prospects of unemployment ahead.

He felt a strange disquiet. In his life he had so far proved to be little better than average. He was unwilling to commit himself to something, like other bright people around him, either to studies or to games. For he could see that there wasn't much to be achieved, however hard one strived. The real power was monopoly of a family. Others were only allowed to make a living at their pleasure and whim.

It was so in India and he found that similar power structure operated more rigorously in Nepal, which unlike India was not a democracy but a monarchy.

Nawin never took part in active politics and even eschewed voting in his college days. But he immediately looked for the political structure operating behind it, whenever he came across a situation. It made him deeply sceptical of the life around. He saw no way in which he could find an opening to begin somewhere, to build his own life. It disheartened him further when he saw that there is no remedy to the problems around except removing it fully and replacing it by something else totally new. But so deeply entrenched was the system over generations that it looked almost impossible to dispose. He was losing interest in making some sort of a career through somehow joining the system.

His thoughts diverted to the responsibilities he had to bear. Anil had joined college. His father had continued to borrow money to meet the expenses. Nawin was expected to help his father as he was too old now to take up new work.

Nawin attended the chemist shop his cousins ran, in order to get engaged in something productive. Once he went to the airport to see off one of his cousins who worked in a government job and went to Kathmandu for a few weeks every year .

The sight of a small aircraft taking off thrilled him. It had earlier landed at the bumpy, uneven track, shaking while it taxied to the weather-beaten, dilapidated building, serving as terminal. On one of the foggy mornings last winter, one such aircraft had crashed in Dhangadi, killing all the people on board, due to poor visibility - people speculated.

Winter in Terai could be severe, Nawin realised that year, when he was practising to take part in the games. The sun appeared only for an hour or two in the evenings. A thick fog enveloped the surrounding area of the town most of the time. If there were rains as well, it could be as cold as in the hills, Nawin thought.

But now it had started to get hotter, and the patients with snake-bites started to arrive at the Zonal Hospital in front of their shop. Some patients died, as they arrived late. They had waited to receive treatment from a *Dhami*, a spiritual priest of their village. They were rushed to the hospital only after their condition deteriorated.

It was a hit and miss, receiving treatment from a *Dhami*. People bitten by non-poisonous snakes survived, to his credit. The ones who died were as per the wish of the almighty. He tried equally hard to save each patient of snake-bite, or other ailments, through his prayers.

Nawin's cousins had a lady-doctor running a clinic at their shop. Her prescriptions generated extra sales. Since abortion was illegal at that time, she quietly performed it at her clinic, at a high charge.

As she was the only woman doctor in the town, her clinic was crowded with female patients. They hesitated to go to a male doctor. If there was no abortion to be performed any day, the doctor looked disappointed. She was not satisfied with the income she earned from the consultations alone.

Nawin decided to go to Kathmandu, when he came to know that a few vacancies had been announced for the job of police officer. In Kathmandu he lived with an acquaintance for some time. On realising that he may have to live like that for several months before he found a job, he along with two other unemployed men who too had graduation degrees like him, from the same university, hired a room. They belonged to the neighbouring villages of his town Ghat, across the river.

They were all competing for the same job of police inspector, or similar available jobs. It was an uneasy partnership, to live together just to keep their expenses at a minimum while vying for the same jobs. Since they were on an equal footing on almost every matter, what made any difference was the connections one had with the powerful people in Kathmandu, (and kept it secret).

On the day he went to submit his application at the police-headquarters, Nawin was told that he was too young - few months short of the desired twenty-years, the minimum age to apply for the job. He felt disheartened. He would be eligible to apply only the next year. His finances were running out.

He tried to get a job in a private company, but did not succeed. He tried to get the job of a teacher, again with no luck. Almost everywhere recommendations were sought, from someone well-established. Nawin knew no one in Kathmandu who could have helped him.

After fourteen years of schooling Nawin found himself lacking in a skill or skills, that could help him become self-employed. He was completely at the mercy of the system. There were many others like him.

Life, at that time, in Kathmandu, was oppressive. Jobs were scarce, like the supplies. Nawin had little privacy and felt crowded, both by his room-mates and by their visitors, who were also unemployed. They all spent time waiting at the residences of the political leaders of their district, Baitadi, in the hope of finding a government job, or any job.

Lokendra Bahadur Chand, from Baitadi, had been the last Prime Minister of Nepal, so his abode was the most frequented. There was an active rule of the king. Police and military jobs were the most rewarding and therefore the most sought after by young graduates like Nawin. But they were very difficult to get, because of undeclared criteria of caste or political affiliations, apart from the regular written and oral examinations, and the checking of the physical fitness. Nawin slowly understood the way things operated. He discovered that even if he waited for a year to compete for the job of a police officer, he still stood no chance.

'To join a force you need a source,' said his room partner, to humour himself in the depressing circumstances, and to the others, visiting him. 'Source' meant some kind of connection with people who knew the ones in powerful positions, in high places.

Civilian jobs were dominated by another caste. Not having a strong political or caste connection left one at a great disadvantage. In addition was the fact that everyone serving in the government was actually serving the king.

There was great political and social turmoil simmering below the surface. A revolution looked imminent, in spite of the heavy-handed ways of the His Majesty's Government (or HMG, as it was popularly called).

There were reports of disappearing activists, the leaders of a possible revolt, in the weekly newspapers published privately. Those periodicals sold out as soon as they appeared on the footpaths, the more radical ones more so – the ones affiliated with a communist party. Actually the publication of the leftist papers was illegal.

Communist leaders faced a greater threat from the system, as they wanted a republic in the country, so most of them were underground; in hiding.

One of the journalists publishing such a radical weekly, Padam Thakurathi, was shot at right in his residence in Old-Baneshwar, very early one winter morning. Rumours circulated that he was shot by snipers of the state. He lost an eye but survived, resuming publication of his paper a few months later, after he received medical treatment abroad.

Siege seemed to live side-by-side with subversion. The revolt stalked authority in a way that it looked if an open confrontation could begin at any movement which would be far too violent than one could imagine.

At times, pamphlets were distributed at Ratna Park and New Road. These areas were not only the heart of the city but were the centre of clandestine activities, frequented by opposition politicians when they were not in jail or underground. Also present there were their supporters, not to mention the spies from the state.

On one occasion a spy disappeared from there and his mutilated body was found in the forest near the cement factory at Chovar. So people knew who were the supporters of the inevitable revolt and who were its enemies.

Idlers too went there, to the New Road area, to read the only legal and state-owned daily newspaper *Gorkhapatra*, free of cost, stuck on the wall of Bhugol park, while eating peanuts in the sun. Next to it was the building where the *Gorkhapatra* was published, before it was distributed all over the country.

Sporadic pamphlet distribution, when it took place, made that evening and the next few days more lively and dramatic. The pamphlets asked the people to revolt against the rule of the king. The pamphlet distributors were often caught by the police and taken away to be tortured. Some of them never returned, particularly those who did not have someone in power to bail them out. The literature of dissent created during that time, without inviting the retaliation of the HMG, like the one of Shakar Lamichane or Parizat, was so discreet that even to this day, people struggle to decipher its meaning.

It was a very exciting time to be around in Kathmandu. Nawin had witnessed nothing of this sort when he was in India.

Life was similar to life in the wilderness, where the strong preyed upon the weak with impunity. Siding with the ones in power was a sure-shot guarantee of survival. Revolt seemed just a day away.

The government controlled information. So the media mostly reported the daily activities of the members of the royal family, or the messages of felicitation the king sent to the leaders in other countries on an important day. Through radio, television or the newspapers such information poured in. In turn, more and more nations backed the proposal of the king to declare Nepal a zone of peace. No one abroad seemed to have sensed the turbulence and violence in Nepalese society.

The only other news published was the felicitations the leaders of the countries like Germany, Norway or Japan sent on the occasion of the king's birthday, reciprocating his gesture.

The king went abroad often on visits to Europe or America. Government servants wore the national-dress to stand in line on the roads the king's motorcade passed through, to see him off. The day when the king left the country on a foreign visit was declared a national holiday. Children also lined the roads clad in their school-uniforms, even if it was raining.

On the day the king returned, the same drill took place for the civil servants and the school-children.

This exercise was also repeated when he went to the airport, to receive the leader of a friendly country visiting Nepal. Or to see them off.

Eventually Nawin landed a temporary job as a lab technician in the veterinary department of the government. By then he had made a few connections with some political leaders and senior bureaucrats from his district in Kathmandu (by visiting their residences regularly over the months, with a request to find him a job).

It was another way to find a government job, albeit temporary, without appearing in a commissioning exam, which was called for only once in a while by the Public Service Commission. In most cases, depending on the mercy of the higher-ups, those temporary jobs became permanent. Though, there were people retiring from a temporary government job without ever becoming permanent, and hence without any pension or other retirement benefits.

Nawin felt immensely relieved to have found a job. Finally he had avoided the possibility of returning home empty-handed, after spending the money his father had borrowed for him to go to Kathmandu, to try his luck to find a job. The thought of remaining unemployed had been a source of a great anxiety since the day he arrived in Kathmandu. Now, however, he could live in Kathmandu on his own, and, maybe, further his career as well, and finally bail his father out of debt and finance the education of Anil.

Once into the temporary job, there was not much to be done, as he soon discovered, and the salary was barely enough to sustain his frugal life. By now he shared a room with another person, similarly employed in the same department. They both cooked in the same room.

The landlord had put a number on each of the ten rooms he had given on hire in the first two floors of his house. The tenants shared a common latrine and a tap connected to the water tank. In the eleventh lived his first wife, who was barren. The landlord lived on the top floor with his second wife (the sister of his first wife) and their son. At the head of stairs to the top floor hung the name-plate of the landlord, with an in/out slider, below his name, as if in an office. Nawin found the eccentricities of the people in Kathmandu intriguing and at times ridiculous.

They lived as if the world outside Kathmandu was non-existent. He assumed that living so close to the power structure which had ruled the country for centuries had made them adopt the mysterious ways of the ruling class, though only a few actually belonged to it. But most of them behaved as if they had a direct connection with the ruler: The king.

This farce was not difficult to see through. Besides the life was as deprived as anywhere else in the country, in terms of education, health and information.

The rituals and superstitions defined the people in Kathmandu too, like they did the people in his native village Dhura. To Nawin it appeared as if a mass hysteria gripped the people perpetually, and they behaved accordingly. The violence of life was enough to make one neurotic.

AUTUMN arrived with the festival of Dashain. It ritually began with a fortnight of fasting, followed by one of feasting. Government offices were closed for ten days, and the city looked deserted as most of the outsiders had gone to their homes, to celebrate the festival.

The affluent native people of Kathmandu seldom left their homes during this period. They played cards with their families or relations and indulged in the orgies of drinking and eating. But there were also the people not so well-off, who couldn't afford to slaughter a castrated male goat, raised for the meat; to celebrate Dashain.

A male goat grown up without castration called *boka* had a distinct stinking smell – alive or when cooked after slaughtering. People drew parallels, including teasing a young man remaining unmarried till late, that he would start stinking like a *boka* if he did not marry soon.

After the slaughter of a castrated male goat, a *khasi*, at the beginning of the festival, by the people who could afford it, the meat was kept in the refrigerator to eat during the fortnight-long festival. During Dashain, the prices of commodities shot up. Supplies of many goods, including vegetables and milk, stopped coming into Kathmandu, as everybody seemed to have stopped working.

People not so well-off bought only a kilogram or two of *khasi*-meat, while the goat's defunct scrotum and pelvic area was on display beside its chopped-off corpse, to prove that there was no foul play, at the Hindu butcher's shop.

Muslim butchers sold *Halal* goat meat, with the skin of the animal removed. But they were not trusted by the natives. For they often also slaughtered a goat or a sheep as well, to mix its meat with the *khasi*-meat. But they had their clientele in a few Bengali families, who came to Kathmandu as refugees during the Bangladesh war. Or there were the migrant Bihari labourers, who liked their meat without skin.

The display of the defunct scrotum of a *khasi* at a butcher's shop was once used by a communist leader Babu Ram Bhattarai as a parallel, for denouncing and equating democracy with selling goat-meat while displaying the scrotum. He wanted a total revolt and a communist rule afterwards. Dictatorship of proletariat as described in communist literature.

A Hindu butcher decapitated a goat using a khukri, a sharp short dagger. He then sat on its headless still-kicking body to collect the blood in a container. Demand for clotted blood was high as it was used to feed a woman who had recently delivered a baby (after frying its jelly-like pieces with different spices in the cooking oil). After the body of the goat stopped kicking, the butcher burned the hair on its skin with a lighted torch. Then he shaved the burnt hair with a blade or a razor.

Then the corpse was slit open at the chest and the inner parts were separated, one-by-one. Its intestine and stomach were cleaned by putting water from one end and then passing it all the way to the other, several times. Lungs, liver, kidney, and heart were all separated and washed, to cater to the demands of different customers. Even the skin was consumed, on which the butcher applied a paste of turmeric, to turn it yellow.

Every part of the *khasi* was thus consumed, including the head (which, after removing the horns and jaws, was cut into small pieces with a big, sharp knife). The head or intestines were sold to a single customer mostly, at a lump-sum which was lower than the more muscular limbs.

The slaughtering and cleaning took place in front of the customers beside the butcher's shop. Customers waited for the butcher to finish. Street dogs watched hungrily and patiently, until they began fighting over scraps hurled towards them, occasionally, by the butcher.

On a day the butcher did not have a helper, his obese wife could be seen helping him slothfully – if he was too busy managing a recent slaughter.

She sold meat to the waiting customers, after chopping it into smaller portions on a platform made of a waist-high tree-stump. She then weighed the meat on a balance, before handing it over to a customer and collecting the money. She too knew the trick of the trade – that muscular parts were to be sold last and the bony ones sold first. Clever customers asked her to do it the other way, inviting some arguments. Every time her knife came down, customers watched to which side went the meat and which side the bones.

At times one could find a customer quarrelling with the butcher on a cold winter morning. He would be holding his young son in one arm while in the other perched a cigarette between his fingers. Once he had brought with him the cooked meat in a cooker to prove that he was sold nothing but bones the previous evening. He gesticulated and smoked alternately, with the hand holding the cigarette, while he argued with the butcher and his son watched on. The butcher somehow assuaged his anger and promised that he will give him only the leg or chest parts the next time, to compensate for the loss.

For some, *khasi*-meat was unaffordable during *Dashain*, when the meat's cost escalated steeply. They managed with the cheaper alternative: poultry or buffalo-meat.

Buffalo meat was sold in an exclusive shop, spread on its floor, after its uncovered carcass dripping with blood was brought there in a rickshaw. The slaughter of buffaloes was made on the banks of either the river Bagmati or Bishnumati. A couple of dozens of buffaloes were slaughtered at a time, by the professionals, before they were loaded in rickshaws to be distributed to different shops in the city. Later in the day, boiled spinal cord or fried tongue of buffalo would be displayed in eateries in the narrow lanes of the city, where the sun seldom penetrated.

In his neighbourhood, Nawin saw a woman teasing her embarrassed neighbour, for she was cooking cheap greens like *rio saag* as usual, instead of the expensive cauliflower and potato, on one of the days of *Dashain* festival. To it, the woman replied with a shy smile that only the day before her family had had cauliflower. So, for a change, they were having greens today.

Women visited a nearby temple in the morning during this period, after they had a bath, wearing their best sari and jewellery, with a plate in their hands, a piece of cloth covering it, masking the offerings they would make at the temple.

The rituals were tiresome lasting a fortnight and expenses were unworthy, for one who could ill-afford them. If it meant somehow climbing the social ladder through building relations it was bearable. For the not so savvy however, escaping the festivals was a choice. A beginning of a menstruation cycle, as soon as the festival started, for one of the women of the household, made a perfect excuse to eschew celebrations. People resorted to it, real or feigned, as per the requirement. A menstruation period of a woman made her entire household unfit to take part in a religious celebration.

It is a different matter that even if used genuinely, relations accepted this news of the beginning of a menstruation cycle with cynicism and sarcasm. And claiming the real reason to be one's unwillingness to celebrate.

Grown-up children gambled, playing *langur-gurja*, with money they had extracted from the elders in their families.

They played on a street-corner where a fellow shook dices in a plastic mug. There was a sheet of card symbols spread in front of him - hearts, spades, clubs and diamonds. He was shouting inviting slogans to entice people to make a bet. People from the crowd around him put their bets on different symbols. He was not happy: he wanted more people to join. He was restlessly looking around to see if a customer was about to come running to him to make a bet. Finally he put the mug on the ground over the dices. But he wanted a few more people in the crowd to make a bet before he exposed the dices and the winners.

Then he lifted the mug and the winning symbols on the dices were exposed. The people in the crowd made various noises. He then hastily collected the money of the losing parties from the sheet in front of him and paid the winners. Then he was ready for the next game; some people left the crowd while some others joined it.

This game was played under the constant threat of the police arriving and arresting the players and the organisers. But police intervention seldom happened, as during this period gambling was allowed as part of the celebrations.

On the day of Dashain, the television channels showed live firstly the king receiving tika from his only surviving elder in the family, the queen mother, his step-mother, exactly at the time declared auspicious by his priests. Then how he in turn gave tika to the queen and the crown-prince, wearing yellow garlands of the sprouts of barley called *jamara* around their necks. By the time his family gave tika to each other, elders to the younger, it was already mid-day.

A crowd composed of the prime minister, the chiefs of the security services, and other governmental bodies waited to receive tika from the king. Also in the crowd were senior bureaucrats from every government department. They were all inside the gates of the royal palace. They gathered there after giving or receiving tika hurriedly, in their homes in the morning, as being late to reach the palace of the king on that day would be counted against them.

And outside the royal palace, at the gates, was a long queue of commoners, as well as a few tourists. They were waiting for the king to become free, after giving tika to the people already inside the gates. It took until evening before the king was free to give tika to the commoners, who were now allowed to enter the royal palace.

At the bottom of stairs several metres high, leading to the palace, stood the king, giving tika to the commoners leaning over a desk placed between them. The king was smiling and talking to a few of them. The queen and the crown-prince also gave tika at other desks in front of the wide stairs, with the palace in the background.

The commoners, separated from the royals by the desk, received tika bowing to the royals, with their hands folded in reverence. It was how Dashain was celebrated, not only by the elders giving tika to the youngsters in a family, but also the stronger to the weaker, the higher officials to the lower.

For the opportunists, it was an occasion to make a career move, notwithstanding the cultural or religious significance of Dashain. Tika being nothing else but a few grains of rice dipped into the paste of red vermilion powder. Put on the forehead of one, it had a much larger symbolic significance.

More so, when one was in the crowd at the royal palace, where people that mattered were present.

Soon after Dashain, the crowd of commoners rushed to a small shop, that of a photographer, on New Road. The owner was the only photographer allowed to take pictures of the king and his family giving tika to the people outside the royal family. By now, photography had turned coloured from black and white.

There were two big rival shops on either side of that small shop. The big shops developed colour pictures from the negatives that their collection centres gathered from various towns across the country. They boasted of automatic processing machines. Workers dressed in white aprons and wearing masks developed, cut and packed the photographs, along with the negatives, to be distributed back to the customers.

The rival shops featured their staff working behind the large glass windows, through which some people looked with interest, making a crowd outside those two shops almost everyday.

It was speculated however, that the small shop situated between them made a much higher profit than those two big shops.

There were posters full of ticket sized pictures of the people, stuck on a wall next to the small shop, with numbers under each picture. The photographs were of people receiving tika from the royals. Most customers ordered enlarged versions of their picture, at an additional charge. It was good to display such a photograph in their workplace or at home.

Receiving tika from the king or another royal was a sign of being close to the royal family and the system ruling the country, which was advantageous when bidding on a government contract or some other business doled out by the government.

For less mercenary people, the photograph was a symbol of tribute to the king, to hang in their homes.

It was also during Dashain that the Chinese government gifted a few hundred sheep to the government of Nepal. It was reported by the *Gorkhapatra*, every year, along with the pictures of the sheep being herded into the office of Nepal Food Corporation at Thapathali.

It was assumed that the sheep were a friendly gift from a rich, neighbouring country, China, to the poor people of Nepal, who were not able to buy themselves meat to celebrate their main festival.

But no one knew what happened to those sheep, because none of the poor ever received them.

It was a similar story with the assistance other friendly countries extended to Nepal. It just remained a news item in the *Gorkhapatra* or Radio Nepal and nothing more. Journalists never made a deeper enquiry into anything and were no better than clerks. But they had a secure government job which offered them opportunities to get training in the best colleges in Europe and the USA. Probably it suited those professors too in those colleges, who trained those journalists, who were on the payroll of a totalitarian government, that they never practised what they learnt.

In short, a large amount of the money coming as foreign developmental aid into Nepal disappeared without a trace in most of the cases. It was speculated that it returned to the country from where it originated, through shoddy consultation fees or bribes. So any enquiry into such matters might have troubled people outside Nepal as well.

Such projects were steadily trapping Nepal as a nation into debts, though the life remained the same for the common man.

If an occasional benevolence unto the most needy created a good feeling among the people about the king, Birendra was clever at creating or performing them. In one instance, he once reportedly drove during the night to Birganj, along with the queen. There must have been royal-guards in other vehicles, before and after his. It was still dark when he reached there.

On arriving the royal couple took a rickshaw for a change, to travel a certain distance. They chatted with the rickshaw-puller like ordinary people and gathered most of the information about his family and life.

Before they left they handed over several thousand rupees to him. Fortunately for him, he did not die of shock, as this amount was more than he would have earned in a year, pulling his rickshaw in the hot weather of Birganj.

This story was leaked to the newspapers, which then featured interviews of the rickshaw-puller, and photographs. He said that initially his passengers spoke like aristocrats, but as it was still dark in the morning he did not recognise the royal couple. Also, they did not identify themselves, even when they left.

This story was also reported by Indian Hindi newspapers on the other side, as Birganj is a border town on the Nepalese side. This incident might have become a part of the folklore, at least in the village where the rickshaw-puller lived, which could as well have been in India.

It was a brilliant public relations exercise, but not necessary, if one considered that the whole machinery of the government in Nepal worked only to create a favourable image of the king.

TENANTS were always changing in the house where Nawin shared a room. Families coming to live there did not stay long, as they found the facilities and privacy limited.

Mostly, students and single men occupied the ten rental rooms of the house. The landlord and his wives preferred to identify the tenants according to their room numbers, instead of the names.

Indeed, as they changed so frequently, it was difficult to remember the names. Their servant also did the same, calling Nawin and his partner 'Number Ten'. He was a supercilious village-boy in his teens who expected to join the police or military service using the connections of the landlord, when he was old enough. Or, somehow, he would be co-opted as a peon in a government office through a relation of his landlord. But, by then, he might have already worked for more than a decade as a domestic help for the landlord. He probably had run away from his home in the hills after it became too much crowded with the siblings his parents bred recklessly, or his father took a second, younger wife, after the death of his mother.

Now, having seen the city, he wanted to have a house here and a car too, through a job in the police or army. He has learnt the language the royals spoke among themselves and the aristocrats of the ruling class imitated, to perfection. It will be his chief qualification to climb up the social ladder and secure a marriage amongst the native families in Kathmandu. He was right in choosing the basic things needed for survival in the capital. Only what he was waiting for was an opening and a little luck.

Getting work with the security services depended on having patrons with connections. On one occasion, a senior police officer was found to be colour-blind, by the foreigners who came to select the ones to serve in the UN Peace-keeping Operations.

They started to come to select them when it was found that the ones earlier selected by the authorities here were found unfit. The UN duty, and the pay it meant, was the main attraction for the people serving in the Nepalese security forces. It earned them enough money to buy a house and a car in the capital, Kathmandu. This dream of a middle-class life in Kathmandu was shared by most in the country. Joining the security forces was the short-cut for those who had no other merits but their connections.

Nawin and his room partner were *dus numbris* of the house, which colloquially meant fraudsters. Even the servant of the landlord and fellow-tenants too smiled at them, calling them by their number, instead of the names.

In the rainy season, which was prolonged in Kathmandu, the soaked roads were full of puddles. Nawin had to make take a zig-zag route through it, jumping over the puddles. Passing vehicles, though very few in number those days, were a constant threat to pedestrians as they would splash water as they passed by.

Finding the idleness at job difficult to cope, Nawin borrowed books from the British Council Library at Kantipath and read them at work. During lunch he went away to have his usual snack of boiled eggs and tea - taking a break from his reading during working hours. He was not convinced of the circumstances around him. The books further aggravated his doubts that life may have more to offer.

Sometime back, the Chernobyl nuclear disaster had taken place in the USSR. A short-time afterwards, rumours spread in Kathmandu that the powdered milk the national dairy used to make milk with, which was then sold in bottles or plastic pouches, was imported from a country near Chernobyl. So it could contain nuclear contamination. People worried over this matter. In fact, they accepted most rumours as truth, as often no explanation was offered by the government in the case of any controversy.

This rumour grew stronger until almost everyone in Kathmandu avoided the milk supplied by the state-owned dairy. They drank lemon or black tea instead. The demand for powdered baby milk made in India or Australia soared. The Nepal dairy might have closed down, if it was not owned by the government.

The demand for local milk coming from the neighbouring villages increased. Vendors on their bicycles brought it to people in the city in two aluminium pitchers tied on both sides of their bicycle measured and poured the milk into the customer's container, after receiving the payment.

At work, occasionally Nawin prepared culture media on a dish, in the laboratory. He put the culture of a poultry liver or lungs in the incubator. The pathogens were isolated. His boss, a Veterinarian, identified the pathogens by mixing various chemical reagents.

He would then ask Nawin to do the antibiotic sensitivity tests. Nawin also supervised the washing and sterilisation of dishes and other equipment. There was a plant to make distilled water and weighing machine to make normal saline or other liquid preparations of different kinds of sugars.

Somehow, very often the media or liquids he prepared caught a contamination, and colonies of fungus appeared in them when cooled. His boss discovered later that the filter which sterilised the air during the processes was not working properly. It was corrected, but the contamination persisted. They concluded that there must also be some problem with the washing. But there was rarely a sample in a week. So it worked on a hit and miss basis. At times the media and the reagents were fine, at others they had to be discarded due to contamination.

Behind the laboratory where Nawin worked were the high walls of Central Prison, which had political detainees too, apart from the criminals. Among them was perhaps Shailaja Acharya, the niece of late B.P. Koirala.

She was a young, unmarried, good-looking woman, who later became a Deputy Prime Minister of the country. She told an interviewer later that she stopped menstruating while in that jail; because she was left to almost starve by the government of the king.

The high walls of this prison were once breached by Ganesh Man Singh, who escaped from there to run away to seek political asylum in India. He later returned to lead a popular uprising in the late 1980s, which finally overthrew the absolute rule of the king.

The Central Prison had the National stadium called Dasrath Rangsala, on the other side. The previous summer a big accident claimed the lives of a hundred or so football fans, who had gathered there to watch a final game between two leading rival local clubs. It was a sultry afternoon of July. Suddenly there was a deluge of hail and strong winds. The sky blackened to the extent that it looked as if it was night.

Nawin was in his room with his partner. He was having black tea after having just returned from his job. They were listening to Radio Nepal. It suddenly broke the news of the accident. It did not elaborate much. But Nawin and his room partner heard the rumour from another tenant that the police had closed all the gates of the stadium after the game started.

It was to keep people without tickets from entering the stadium, while policemen themselves watched the match. The bad weather turned worse. There was no roof in the stadium except on the western VIP part, which was not connected to the rest of the stadium. So the people couldn't go there to take shelter.

The panicked crowd of nearly twenty-five thousand ran towards the only open south gate, when the exceptionally heavy hailstorm began hitting them. The consequent stampede caused the tragedy.

The king visited the Bir hospital the same night, to take stock of the injured, the radio also reported, later in a special bulletin. Nawin remembered that it rained till late into the night that day.

That winter an earthquake shook the valley. It was around midnight. Every tenant of Nawin's house, jolted awake, ran to the open space outside the house. The landlord and his family took longer, as they had to come down from the top-floor. Soon all the neighbours were out and the street was overcrowded. Everyone waited for almost an hour, fearing aftershocks, before returning to their rooms.

The next day brought news that thousands of people had died in remote villages, when their ill-made houses collapsed during the earthquake. Those deaths were mostly in the eastern part of the country, a remote area many days' walk away from any road. The number of casualties kept increasing for the next several days, as it took time for news to reach from the very remote villages. In Dharan, a town in the east, nearly a quarter of all the houses collapsed, as it was very close to the epicentre of the quake.

In the following weeks tents, blankets and clothes arrived from various countries across the world, along with packaged food and water, at the Tribhuwan International Airport in Kathmandu.

It was for the victims of the earthquake. But the rumours doing the rounds were that very little of it was reaching the actual victims. Government employees and the police at the airport stole most of it. Given their low salaries, they were only a little better than the earthquake victims, and hence the rumour was plausible, Nawin thought, thinking about his own situation and job.

There appeared also that winter, photocopies of a British newspaper report, reporting that the Nepalese Crown-prince Dipendra was expelled from the elite Eton school in England, for trying to sell liquor and drugs in the school, to muster some extra cash. There was apparently a limit on what his parents could give him, as pocket money, at Eton. The prince was also reported to have claimed that he could bed any girl he wanted, in Nepal.

Carrying this report could have been seditious in Nepal, but many people had a copy of it. Nawin had one. He kept it in a file, to show it to only his close friends. It was heard afterwards, that the prince was allowed to continue his education after receiving warnings.

But he returned to Kathmandu permanently sometime later, without having completed his education - people speculated. The younger royals routinely took drugs and alcohol, one often heard. There were only rumours floating around about the royals never hard or harsh facts about their true lives or selves; the media would project them favourably, hiding all faults, making them appear too good to be human.

Idleness was disheartening to Nawin, as were the things happening around. Life seemed to be going nowhere, dwindling to a routine where the feeling of loss was overbearing. Nawin jogged several kilometres each morning, then had a bath and prepared the food for himself and his room partner, before they went to their respective offices. His partner was a late-riser, and prepared the evening meals.

In winter it was always foggy in the mornings in Kathmandu. As Nawin jogged, he saw very few people on the roads apart from the ones selling vegetables on baskets hanging from their shoulders or milk from pitchers on their bicycles. Cold water evaporated off his warm body as Nawin bathed in the morning in the open, after jogging.

In winter, his room-partner had a bath only on Saturdays, the weekly holidays. He would watch, shivering, as vapour rose off Nawin's body. He warned Nawin that he would fall sick for bathing with cold water on such cold mornings. Nawin told him that he was a sportsman, and was physically tough.

Despite being in a similar situation, Nawin found his room-partner far more assured than he himself was. He rose late and leisurely went about his daily life. He was relaxed and cool when he dealt with friends who came to visit him. He often went to visit them. It appeared to Nawin that he had connections with some really important people.

Nawin had almost no friends to go to in Kathmandu. Even the connections he had made with influential people he did not bother to consolidate. His restlessness made him seek education through books and build his fitness through exercise. But, at times, these appeared to him to be futile, as what mattered was having connections or influential relations. He then was gripped by long periods of silent melancholia which lasted hours or days, speaking even to his partner only if it was necessary, though sharing the food and living space with him.

He contemplated and tried to look into the future. He could not see far. The restlessness returned. He had taken admission for the master's degree in Sociology at Tribhuwan University, Kirtipur. In one such mood he decided to drop out. He had discovered that to study this kind of subject by attending regular classes was of no use. More so because the teachers were often absent and students never tired of discussing politics.

He was still thinking of competing for the job of an army or police officer the next year, or to even appear in the civil service examination for a permanent job. Keeping his body fit was necessary, Nawin thought, as was educating himself, for the future looked so uncertain.

His aversion to meat-eating returned often and lasted for months. There also was a constant fear in Kathmandu that as often as not the *khasi*-meat being served in a restaurant was actually the cheaper alternative: buffalo-meat. So that was another reason for him to avoid meat.

Most people migrating to Kathmandu adapted. They ate buffalo-meat, as it was easily and cheaply available in the eateries of the city. Likewise, they also started to eat beef once they migrated out of the country.

Nawin was unable to become so pragmatic. He often informed his father with pride, in his letters or when he visited home, that he had never eaten buffalo-meat knowingly in Kathmandu. To his amusement, Nawin discovered many years later that the high caste Hindu leaders of communist parties often claimed to have eaten buffalo-meat, to present it as a proof that they were real communists.

During his visits home, his father asked him to get married. He said he was getting a few proposals from the parents of suitable girls of their caste. Dev had become hopeful after Nawin sent him a small amount of money regularly, saved from a meagre salary after living a frugal life. He had observed that Nawin was a responsible young man and would take care of the family after him. But Nawin didn't feel settled given his present circumstances. So marriage was simply out of the question. He wanted to change jobs to earn more. But there were hardly any openings he could foresee.

On days he did not go to jog, Nawin went walking to a Buddhist monastery on the top of a hillock, in the evening. It was near his house. Obscenities were written on the walls of the monastery and genitals were drawn with chalk.

The caretaker of the monastery frequently removed these marks with a wet piece of cloth, only to see them reappear. There was a warning painted on the walls prohibiting people from either taking drugs or indulging in immoral activities there, for it was a religious shrine.

Nawin often saw the caretaker pouring used up lubricant procured from an automobile workshop on the big flat stones on which the visitors sat. It was obviously to keep them away. But rains washed the lubricant away quickly enough. When the caretaker was not around, young couples could be seen sitting together, holding hands and talking intimately, or groups of young men smoking drugs and talking in a subdued manner.

Some people came there to offer prayers, but the beautifully carved wooden doors and windows of the monastery were often closed. If they could not enter, they folded their hands from the outside facing the monastery, to offer their prayers, and then spilled the grains of rice they had brought with them, to the pigeons; after calling: '...Aa...Aa...Aa.'

The waiting pigeons on the nearby roofs of the houses, or from electric cables or poles or trees, would fly down in droves, raising a lot of dust and dropping some of their feathers. They would feed quickly on the scattered rice grains, which the devotees would watch with great satisfaction.

Then someone inevitably came climbing the stairs from behind, disturbing the feeding pigeons. They flew away to the places they came from, again raising a lot of dust. Their droppings were a constant threat to the people walking on the road below the electric cables. They also littered the monastery walls and the surroundings with their droppings.

An old woman watched this spectacle impassively from one of the many windows of her house. She had purchased some milk from a vendor down on the street, in a container with a lid, tied by a rope she was slowly pulling upwards. She was possibly too old to go down the stairs and then climb back with the milk. She dropped the money from the window after receiving her milk, which the vendor collected from the ground.

Nawin felt hostile towards those pigeons, so well-fed by the devotees and considered a bird of peace by the people. Their continuous raising of dust often chased him away from the monastery, where he had gone for some solitude and fresh air. He wished that the people started eating them - particularly the ones who considered themselves devotees, by feeding them, instead of the poultry - which they consumed routinely. After all, both the species were the same, if one considered them in terms of their being a source of meat.

In winter there was the birthday of the king, just a few days before the New Year day of the Gregorian calendar. Around this time the night temperatures dropped to below zero in Kathmandu. The king's birthday was celebrated by the government in every major town of the country. Processions of vehicles adorned with flower garlands, and red-coloured sheets were taken out.

The vehicles carried huge garlanded pictures of the king and the queen atop them, ahead of the processions.

Government officials and local politicians took part in the celebrations, apart from the ones who were also benefiting from the government in some ways. However, there were also a few who genuinely liked the king, in those processions.

On this day the government declared awards and medals in different categories. Half the awards were distributed among the royal family itself, including their personal servants or cooks. The rest were given to the government officials and officers in the security forces. Among the few remaining people receiving those medals were the political activists, writers or journalists on the side of the system.

On this day that year, the much awaited rise in the salary of the government employees too was announced: a flat hundred rupees a month, for every employee, whether a peon or a secretary.

Nawin could not see his future in this system.

He felt it was not only tyrannical but also exploitative, under-employing people at a less than liveable wage. The favoured ones were given chances to serve in the positions where there was an extra income through bribes. Others were left to simply wane and rot away.

But there came an opportunity for Nawin. A pharmaceutical company manufacturing veterinary medicines was hiring in India. Nawin was qualified, as he had a bachelor's degree in biology and chemistry. He went to Ahmadabad and resigned by telegram from his ad hoc government job (which began to appear to him like a cul-de-sac), to take up the job of a business representative for that company in Nepal. At least with the private company there were possibilities. But, still, the next time he went to see his father, his father lamented that private jobs could never be as secure as the government ones.

Dev thought that somehow he will manage. He was feeling his age by now. He persuaded Nawin yet again to get married, as a suitable match was available. Nawin asked his father to wait for a year, as he wanted to first settle down in his new job.

Dev and Nisha were as busy as ever, taking care of Dinesh, but there were few signs of improvement. Somehow, Dinesh had picked up how to dance. The marriage processions often passed through the town, with the pipers playing the folk tunes of romance or chivalry; which the drums, with their rhythmic beats, made more dramatic.

A pair of male dancers called Chhaliya, in their colourful long skirts, pyjamas and turbans and their faces made up with colours holding a shield and a sword each in their hands, while dancing - created a scene of fighting, like in ancient times - in sync with the music. They also sang in between their dance. The bazaar of the town was a place for them to showcase their talent, as people from different villages came there everyday.

A pair of good Chhaliyas was like a celebrity for the people in the area, and high in demand for performing in the marriage-ceremonies. Their fee was higher than the ordinary dancers. It is from them perhaps, that Dinesh had picked up dancing, Nawin thought. He jumped in the middle of a marriage procession and danced, holding the attention of even the real dancers, when the sudden fast beating of the drum gave the cue.

Nawin's brother Anil had qualified for admission to a technical school in a town Panar, which was higher in the hills, than Almora, where Nawin had gone to school. There was a need to pay for his expenses. Nawin did not feel disheartened on finding his father criticising his private job. He knew that the government job he had left would never have given him any chance to help his family financially. And such help from his side was direly needed then.

ON returning to Kathmandu, Nawin found that a family had come to live in room five on the ground floor.

It was Dilip's family. He was also a native of Nepal. But Dilip had lived most of his life in Bombay, where his elder brother worked in a private company, after their father's death.

His brother was much older to Dilip and had a son Dilip's age. His name was Rajesh. Rajesh and Dilip went to college together. After emergency had been called by the Indira Gandhi led government, Rajesh was being summoned to the principal's office, where the teachers put pressure on him to get his father sterilised. His father came to know of it and felt harassed. In fact, his company too was asking him to get sterilised, as they too were under similar pressure.

His brother decided to leave the country. He resigned his job and left Bombay. With the money he had in his provident fund he bought a small piece of land near Dhangadi, where he and his wife soon established a small business selling goods of daily needs. But they kept Rajesh and Dilip in Bombay, asking them to look for a job and also complete their studies. They sent them money till both of them were able to get small jobs that just about paid their bills. But, somehow, Rajesh got trapped in a situation where he was sterilised. He felt very disheartened. Dilip consoled him with great difficulty.

Rajesh decided to leave Bombay and complete his studies at Dhangadi. So Dilip lived with a relation till he completed his studies after Rajesh left.

He thought about seeking a career in Bombay and lingered on there. Now he shared his one room apartment with another person like him, who also was a migrant and did a small part-time job. At times Dilip did two shifts of work to manage his expenses, as life was expensive in Bombay and wages meagre.

The area they lived in was crowded with people like them made filthier due to the mess created by the children of some of the families living there. The authorities had built in the middle of it a two floored concrete building which was full of many latrines and had an adequate supply of water. But there was a charge of a rupee to use it. People with many children couldn't afford and they soiled the surroundings. Dilip thought about hiring an apartment with better living conditions. But the cost was prohibitive.

His brother wanted him to get married, as he wanted him to have children which his son Rajesh could no longer have. He arranged his marriage to a woman in Dhangadi and Dilip got married during a brief ceremony. He stayed with his wife at his brother's house in Dhangadi for a week, before he returned to Bombay to his job.

He found that Rajesh had abandoned studies and had started to help his father in the business. His father wanted him to get married. He had found a barren woman for him to marry, who was abandoned after being briefly married. But Rajesh declined.

Dilip discovered that he wouldn't be able to get a proper job in Bombay as his education was not adequate. Also, he wanted to join a government job which was possible only in his own country. After some time Dilip returned permanently to Dhangadi. Then he came to Kathmandu to find a job.

Dilip and his wife had a new-born son. Dilip worked at a well known hotel in Kathmandu as an accountant.

He wanted to join the civil services as soon as possible. However, every time he appeared in the civil-services examination he dropped-out when he had to sit for the 'Panchayat' exams, though he attempted other subjects.

'Panchayat' addressed the virtues of a party-less democracy, in which every politician was a 'Panch', be it a village-leader or the prime minister. This system was what was ruling the nation at that time, under the king. Stretching the definition further, the ruling class had begun to define every Nepali as a 'Panch' and every 'Panch' as a Nepali.

Obviously, this exam was to test the level of ideological inclination of an examinee. Dilip, with his Bombay education, felt so rebellious against the system that for three years in succession he failed to appear in the examination of 'Panchayat.' He was an avid reader of English novels and a regular subscriber to *The Times of India*, one of the leading English newspapers of India.

It was his wont to quote something in English, when he saw himself losing an argument or when he ran out of words while explaining something.

When they became friendly after a few weeks of acquaintance, Dilip disclosed to Nawin his aversion to the Panchayat system, and said that he was simply not able to read the subject. Therefore he may have to forget his ambition of joining the civil services, he added ruefully.

There was something compulsive about his nature. One night, when his wife and son had gone away to his in-laws for a month, Nawin found him outside the door of the first wife of the landlord, who lived in room number eleven. The room was next to Nawin's room.

Dilip was drunk and was uttering obscenities while softly knocking at the door. He looked embarrassed to be discovered there by Nawin at that late hour, and immediately returned without a word to his own room. Nawin decided to ignore what he had seen.

Nawin felt comfortable at his new job. He gave up his ambitions of joining a government job. He earned more money, and could send some home. He moved out of his shared room and rented an apartment in the middle of the town, sharing it with another man in the same profession.

They had separate rooms but shared a common kitchen, bathroom and sitting room. From the apartment it was easier to make sales calls on customers, as it was centrally located.

Also, no longer was he called *Dus Numbri*.

ONE day Dilip phoned Nawin. He said he got his phone number after a lot of difficulty and he wanted to visit his apartment the next evening. Nawin was glad to hear from him after so many months. He gave Dilip directions to reach a grocery shop in his neighbourhood and said he would meet him there at five the next evening.

He waited for him, and was glad to see him coming, descending a steep road on the left side.

'It is so nice to see you! ... After such a long time!' Dilip said on approaching.

'Yes. How are you? Still working at the same hotel job?' asked Nawin.

'No. I left that soon after you shifted. Now I am working as a journalist in an English-weekly newspaper.'

'I see. How are your wife and son?'

'Oh, they are fine. They have gone to visit my in-laws. My son is on summer vacation from school.'

'Don't you visit your in-laws some time?' asked Nawin.

'I do. But if I stay on for long I find my murderous instincts taking over me, particularly when they force me to eat more than I need to, challenging me if I have become old. I mostly do not brush my teeth till late in the day to avoid their food and only have tea when they force me, saying that I never have food without brushing. Then I slip out to the market and return late in the evening, after having food with some drinks at a hotel.'

Nawin was gripped by a fit of laughter.

'The depression I feel after meeting them lasts for many months,' Dilip added.

'What happened to your civil services exam project?'

'You know that I could have passed them only if I was able to attempt the "Panchayat" paper. Now I have stopped preparing for it. It seems it will not be long before the system is overturned. Anyway, Shelley said that poets are unacknowledged legislators of the world.'

Nawin noticed that Dilip was wearing a small cylindrical charm in his neck tied by a black thread. 'What is it you are wearing?' he asked touching it.

'Oh. Don't touch. I have to keep it in cow's milk for a night if someone other than my family touches it. Recently a doctor I was seeing for an illness I was suffering from for the past few months gave it to me. You know the doctor had been educated in England. But he follows the teachings of an Indian Guru. Several times a year he leaves his medical practice to attend the meditation sessions of the Guru, at times lasting for two weeks, in various religious towns of India.

'He gave me this charm when he found that the medicines he prescribed were not having any effect. He claimed that it is a *Mrityunjaya* (death-winning) charm. He said even if my motorbike hits a car I would not be harmed. He challenged me to try it.'

'I don't believe it. How could a doctor educated in England have faith in all this?' Nawin said incredulously.

'Oh. You are far too rational Nawin. You do not know. That doctor treats most of his patients with his charms. He is becoming so popular that many of the leading politicians, industrialists and movie-stars have started coming to him. I can tell you that from the day I am wearing this charm I am feeling better. The restlessness and insomnia I used to suffer have disappeared. Now I too am a follower of the Guru. There is a big poster of him in my room. My wife has also started to believe in his powers.'

Nawin was not convinced. But he said nothing further. He guessed the lack of success in finding a suitable job had turned Dilip superstitious. Nawin decided to take Dilip to his apartment.

The pager Dilip was carrying rang. He removed it from his belt and read the message. 'It is from an advertisement company working for my newspaper. They want me to call them back. Where is your phone?' Dilip asked. Nawin pointed to a corner of the drawing room. Dilip talked for a long time. He sounded persuading at times while arguing at others. He finally finished.

'They wanted to know if we will publish an advertisement from a coffee shop in the tourist area Thamel, where the tourists frequent and local English papers have a good demand. The shop will not pay us any money but will offer "A free cup of steaming coffee" to the readers who went there with a cutting of their advertisement in our weekly. But I want them to pay us some money as well. You see how difficult it is to work as a journalist,' Dilip said with a tinge of self-pity.

To change the topic Nawin said, 'You still are using a pager. Mobile phones are available now.'

'But a call from a mobile costs five times more than a landline call. Also, you have to pay to receive calls on it. So long as government has a monopoly in telecommunications, the cost will be exploitative. When did you get your landline phone, by the way?' Dilip asked.

'Very recently. Nearly one year after I submitted the application for it.'

'See! What did I tell you. You should have told me earlier. I got my phone within a week. I know many ministers personally. Being a journalist has its advantages,' Dilip boasted, a little vindictively.

The talks inevitably led to politics.

'You know about the multi-million dollar loan the government is trying to negotiate from the Asian Development Bank, to improve the water supply in Kathmandu?' Dilip asked. 'Only if they made rain-water harvesting mandatory for every household in Kathmandu would the water supply improve. You have forty percent of the water supplied lost due to leakage in the pipes placed during the Rana-period. Only if they repaired the pipelines, there will be no need to build the new project with ADB loan. But if there are no new projects there will be no kick-backs for the bureaucrats and the politicians. The donors like ADB do not know that they are the source of corruption here, apart from the lack of development.

'Most of the money they will give as loan will go back to the developed countries, as foreign consultants will be employed at a very high salary. Even if the project is completed, it will be at a much higher cost than the normal. It is like trapping a country into debts to enslave the future generations.'

Nawin smiled. 'Do not worry. The donors are smart enough to know where their money is going. You have not changed. I see the same angry man.' Nawin added as an after-thought. 'After all, you have lived most of your young life in Bombay, where Amitabh Bachchan too lives, making his Bollywood movies, and punishing the villains.'

Dilip laughed and produced a big cucumber wrapped in a newspaper. 'Here, I brought it thinking we will eat it together. Where is your room-partner?'

'He has gone home on leave. I am all alone now, in this big apartment. I will wash this cucumber and we will enjoy it with green chilli and salt. You wait here a while,' Nawin said as he went towards the kitchen.

Dilip followed Nawin, turning his head quickly to look around, instead of remaining in the sitting room. 'You have so many rooms. I am still living in the same room with my wife and son. You know, I have screwed most of the women in the neighbourhood, including the barren who lived next to you, at room number eleven.'

Nawin was shocked. The faces of those women floated across his mind. 'You have so much of space here.' Dilip said. 'Don't you have some adventure?' he laughed.

Nawin's face turned white. He felt envious.

'Yes. I have a girl-friend,' he lied. 'And I hire a TV and VCR often to watch porn movies at night. I just cannot go to a small room of Asan market, to sit with a smelly crowd of villagers from the outskirts, to watch it for a small fee.'

They returned to the sitting room with the cucumber cut in pieces on a plate. Salt in a paste of green chilli was on another plate. They rubbed the paste on the piece of cucumber they ate.

'I dream of writing an English novel. As you know I read widely and am now practising writing in my job as a journalist. Do you think I could do it?' Dilip asked.

Nawin reluctantly replied, 'Why not? If you tried you certainly could.'

'You know, if I write my book my hero will have the power of a wrestler and the sensitive face of an actor. He will not have to force a smile at a particular angle to make dimples on his cheeks, but they will naturally occur whenever he smiles.

'He could lift a car, if the need be, with a rope, from an accident site. He will also be fast enough to get out of the way if a bullet is fired at him. He will have sex with only the most beautiful girls, and make them all have an earth-shaking orgasm. They will fall in love with my hero, but he will never have sex twice with the same girl.'

Dilip was breathless with excitement.

'He will be the next James Bond!' Nawin finally said, with more than a hint of sarcasm. 'And an enemy of feminists as well, for making them have an orgasm every time!! So you can start writing a series, and produce the new titles industrially. Only a little twisting of the plot or theme will make a new book. Isn't it so?'

Dilip appeared unfazed. 'No. James Bond undresses himself for every girl he meets. My hero will not be like that,' he said without any hint of irony. Then he fell silent for a while. The sarcasm had dampened him a little.

But not much. After thinking for a while he said, 'I have already thought about the cover of the book. You know, it will have a man with his face to the readers, running, wearing a suit, with a gun in his hand. A black convertible is chasing him. An aeroplane is flying over him. While on a side on the cover a beautiful girl with pity in her eyes is watching.

'You know what Oscar Wilde had said once. Only artists can make something more golden than gold ...' After hesitating for a while, he asked Nawin, 'What do you think, how would that look?'

Nawin had withdrawn again. 'It will look good. I wonder where you find the literary quotes you use?'

Encouraged, Dilip said, 'Oh, my quotes are from the papers like *The Times of India*. There is a new one everyday on top of the editorials, except on Sunday when there are no editorials. You know, there are many people like me who have a book in their mind. Most of them are working as journalists in different English newspapers. They all say that they want to write a trilogy, instead of a single novel. I am thinking of doing a feature on them. There will be their big coloured pictures in the middle pages of my weekly, with their words on the book they will write in the future.

'I know you too write letters to the editors, in English newspapers,' Dilip continued. 'I read them whenever they appear. At times you write well, but mostly it is ordinary. The short stories you publish are libidinous and suggestive of the lack of sex in your life. After all watching those porn movies and visiting prostitutes in Thamel once in a while is not enough. You should think of getting married. It will help you in getting rid of the influence of comics and Hollywood movies from your stories,' Dilip went on, almost avenging.

Nawin felt more defensive than angry.

Dilip told him later, after the talks drifted through different topics, as the evening progressed, cooling off their hostility to each other, of how he found a middle-aged woman in the neighbourhood peeing while standing, without spoiling her sari; with her young grandson tied to her back.

'If it was not for the sound of water dropping, I might never have known what that woman was doing, standing close to the boundary wall on the other side, while I was enjoying the winter-sun on my side. She was bending a little forward with her legs spread under her sari – which was lifted a little.' Dilip got up to act out what he had witnessed, making Nawin choke with laughter.

'I confirmed it, when she went inside her house, that she had peed. The ground she was standing on was wet. I have never seen a woman doing it standing, though I have lived all my life in Bombay. It seems as if only the women of Kathmandu are capable of it,' Dilip winked.

The talks came back to politics. Dilip, as usual, had an opinion on almost everything. He was also angry about the donors providing money to the Nepalese government to run airlines or buses, as he said it killed the initiative of the private entrepreneurs to invest in transportation. The trend was such in most service-industries, according to Dilip.

Dilip had recently been to Pokhra, sent there when the prime minister was there to take part in a festival organised by the businessmen of the town to attract more tourists. People in this tourist town were enterprising. They had recently started the participation of tourists in a rice plantation ceremony.

It was celebrated only by local farmers, earlier. They drank and feasted and danced in the fields after the rice-plantation during monsoon. Now tourists too joined them and it was widely reported in the local media. The PM was in town to inaugurate the ceremony.

Dilip found the town as crowded as Kathmandu and the water of the fabled Lake Fewa was muddy. Also a wild grass had grown across which covered most of the lake, making the lake unsuitable for boating.

Dilip was surprised to find that most sites of tourists' attraction could be accessed only through properties of locals. Only a guide knew the way and an entry fee had to be paid to see the site after crossing a private property to reach it. He found that there were a few religious sites too of this nature. It was to attract domestic tourists. Dilip decided not to see the temples which can be seen only with the help of a guide and after crossing a private property. However, there was a crowd of Indian tourists seen near those temples, apart from a few domestic ones.

Nawin laughed about it, when Dilip told him this story. He said that he had a memory of Pokhra he had seen many years ago. Then people of the town had not cared much about the tourists except a few taxi drivers and hotel owners. It was a sparsely populated town with houses between fields full of crops. The people he met had very relaxed and pleasing manners.

Dilip rose from the chair and said as it was getting late he had to leave.

'I forgot to offer you even tea,' Nawin said, walking him to the gate of the house to see him off.

'Forget the tea!' Dilip said with his mysterious smile, and shook hands and left.

He phoned a week later and asked if he could bring a woman to Nawin's apartment, to have sex. Dilip offered that if he wished, Nawin could share her. 'I have talked to her about you and she has agreed. Let us have some fun,' he said persuasively.

Nawin decided to lie. 'My partner has returned from his leave with his wife. She will live here for a few weeks. Sorry, it is not possible.'

Dilip said bye in a sad voice, and did not call Nawin for a long time afterwards.

Nawin now thought he was ready for marriage. His father wrote to him about a suitable match.

He at times thought of marrying a girl from Kathmandu itself. He found them to be good-looking and amiable. He tried to court a few of them. But he found that they were not interested. Not only were his looks ordinary, his personality and manners were not impressive either. Whenever he talked to them he fell into an argument or disagreement. Most young women in Kathmandu found it a distinct turn-off.

Nawin had grown up in a very different culture. He perceived the relationship between a man and a woman in a different way than that of the Kathmandu women he tried to court.

He was alarmed at the way the women in Kathmandu wanted to rebel against the hitherto prevalent cultural stereotype of a Nepalese woman. They were as dependent on their parents or husbands as ever, financially, to truly rebel against them. And on the earnings of others they wanted to live a luxurious life with occasional holidays in a European city.

He however, also found that the educated and financially self-sufficient women were less interested in such a kind of rebellion.

He couldn't see how those rebellious women he met could become a wife and a mother of a man like him, who had to earn his living through hard work and a disciplined life. The modernity they often displayed in the liberal way they drank alcohol in a party or their interest in casual sex, was alien to Nawin.

He was doing an ordinary job with a very limited income and didn't have a house of his own. So his courtships only reminded Nawin of his limitations as a desirable man to a woman from Kathmandu.

He felt a little bitter about it. The education which he thought had enabled him to be in a job and the position he had, so far away from his home - as one of his assets - was almost ignored by the women he tried to court.

He always felt that there is a woman for every man in the world who meets his temperament in every manner. If they met by chance and worked together they had the potential to achieve anything. But there was no woman he had met so far who shared his ideas. Most of them wanted a secure marriage in which the only responsibility they wanted to share was to breed a brood. Just like a happy ending in a movie.

Nawin attracted the attention of a few elderly people he met through his friends and acquaintances. They were natives of Kathmandu and had daughters of suitable age to marry. But soon caste considerations came in the way. Also Nawin had to go a long way before he established himself financially. Marriages mostly were a means to climb higher in the social status for most of the people.

A few others who wanted to keep such criteria aside, and marry their daughter with Nawin, wanted him to join their family as a *ghar-jamai.* Becoming a *ghar-jamai* was a very dishonourable position for Nawin, as in it he was expected to cut off relations with his own family and become an adopted son of the family of his wife and in-laws.

He was too proud to accept such a position. He thought that only a destitute or an orphan could accept such a marriage, with a chance that there was a major defect in the character or physique of the woman one was marrying.

The amount of formality and hypocrisy around marriage made him view it with distaste. It made him look more cynically at life. At times he wondered if he had become too old for marriage.

When his father persuaded him through his letter once again to get married, he yielded. His father wrote that the girl he had in mind for Nawin lived in a village near Sora, the town where Nawin studied in the college and went often during his childhood with his parents. Her name was Aarti and she had just entered the same college where Nawin had studied. She had an elder sister who was already married. Her parents ran a small business of ready-made clothes in Sora.

Aarti's father was the nephew of a friend of Dev, who had served with Dev in the British-Indian army during the war. They were reluctant to have their daughter married off to a faraway place like Kathmandu, to a man who was not an Indian. But Dev's friend convinced them that they were finding a good match in Nawin. Dev and his friend belonged to a generation when the British ruled India and the people of Nepal and India were considered the same in the area. They inter married without such considerations of nationality. They also thought that since they spoke the same language and ate the same food, once the marriage took place, any remaining differences due to the separate nationality too could be bridged.

However, Nawin was not sure if he earned enough to maintain a family. That autumn he went home and got married to Aarti. It was a celebration in which the chhaliyas were hired. Dinesh got an opportunity to dance as much as he liked. Anil too attended it, coming down from the technical school in Panar, where he was studying.

Nawin stayed home for a week's honeymoon period with his wife. They went to the different religious places on either side of the border during this time to take a darshan, at times walking to cross the hills, at others to take a bus to travel the distance of a few miles. Then he returned to Kathmandu, leaving his wife with her parents at Sora, as it was two years later only that she was expected to complete her graduation.

RAJIV Gandhi, the Indian Prime Minister, had for some political reasons closed the borders with Nepal except at two points. This led to a lot of hardship for the people living in the bordering area and in the hills in Nepal.

As for Nepal, the only viable access to the sea was through India. The East-West highway in Nepal, called Mahendra highway, was being built by India near its border. It was not complete even after two decades.

So to reach from one part of Nepal to another, one had to enter into India to again enter back into Nepal at another point. This situation was debilitating for the economical development of Nepal. This World Bank financed highway was earlier contracted to China, one heard. Also that, showing the security concerns, India put pressure on Nepal to get this project.

The blockage of free road access to Nepal from India happened, as people talked, after the South Asian Association for Regional Co-operation (SAARC) conference meet took place in Kathmandu. During which the king had a personality clash with Rajiv Gandhi.

For the preparation of the SAARC conference, several weeks before the foreign leaders arrived, the security checks started. Buses were stopped ten kilometres away from the city at Thankot Check-post and were subjected to strict security checks, along with their passengers.

Nawin also noticed that the front part of several buildings at major crossings in the city had been brought-down by the government, using bulldozers, to make the roads wider as a preparation for the SAARC meet. The owners of those truncated buildings were busy covering the damage to their property.

It was also rumoured that Sonia Gandhi, the wife of Rajiv, was denied entry into Pashupatinath temple because she was a Christian. That infuriated Rajiv even further.

Nawin's work took him frequently in and out of Kathmandu. To call on the clients, who were more in number outside Kathmandu. They were either livestock and poultry farmers or the veterinarians. He was regularly frustrated by the security arrangements of the government for the SAARC meet. He had to make extra payment to get into the city after taking a taxi, after being dropped ten kilometres away at the checkpoint.

He was really thankful, when the conference concluded.

Economical sanctions put in place by India against Nepal remained, even when Rajiv Gandhi was ousted from the PM's office. They led to an acute shortage of petroleum products in the country. Indian-made goods also became scarce.

SAARC was said to be the brainchild of King Birendra and the Bangladeshi Dictator General H.M. Ershad. When SAARC was first proposed, Indira Gandhi was said to have expressed a reservation that it will become a forum for the neighbours of India to gang-up against it.

Hosting one of SAARC's periodic meets did not prove to be so propitious for King Birendra, as he picked up an ego clash with Rajiv Gandhi. Most of the leaders of the countries of the region, participating in it, including King Birendra himself, were killed violently, in the aftermath of the Kathmandu SAARC meet. Such was the dynamics of the politics of the region.

Nawin now visited his home more frequently, as his father had expected. He discovered that when alone in Kathmandu, he longed for the intimate moments he had with his wife while at home.

He at times thought of bringing his wife along with him to Kathmandu. She could have attempted her college exams after studying privately at home too. But he was on tours most of the time. He didn't want his wife Aarti to live alone when he was away. Kathmandu was a city and criminal activities were common.

Also, once he hired an entire flat to live with his wife, the expenses would escalate, he thought. In the present job he was not making enough money. He was looking for a change. He had a few friends who worked in the Nepalese pharmaceutical companies, which were a big success recently and offered decent salaries to their employees.

After more than a year of marriage Nawin was told by Aarti that she was expecting a baby, during one of his visits to her to her parents' house. Nawin thought it was too early. He wanted Aarti to terminate her pregnancy. He hoped to take her away to Kathmandu to fulfil the sexual fantasies he had in his mind, before she became pregnant. The presence of a child would take away most of the adventure of sex, Nawin thought.

So far they had not found the desired privacy either at Ghat or Sora to try them. They remained always crowded by visitors and family.

Nawin wasn't prepared for fatherhood yet. But Aarti was already too attached to the foetus growing in her womb to think about an abortion. She simply rejected Nawin's proposal. Nawin was in no position to further insist on that matter. Since she was still living with her parents she was as independent minded as ever. Nawin only gave her a little money for her pocket expenses when he visited her.

Just after her exams the next summer Aarti delivered a healthy boy at the district hospital Sora. Her parents took good care of her.

On getting this news Nawin rushed home to perform the various ceremonies that ensued. It all took place at the home of Aarti's parents at Sora. Nawin's suggestion to take her and the baby to Ghat was declined by Aarti's parents as she was still weak to travel and take care of the child at Ghat.

Nawin's father too attended the functions. He was very happy to have a grandson who was named Rahul in the ceremony. Now until the baby grew up a little, he could not take them to Kathmandu, Nawin thought.

He found that Aarti's parents were a little disappointed to find that Nawin hadn't planned for his life together with his wife after marriage. They were happy to keep Aarti with them till she completed her studies. But their expenses escalated after she became pregnant. They expected Nawin to pay for those expenses.

Aarti had sensed her parents' current thoughts and feelings. She was also aware that of late their business was not doing well. She asked if Nawin had enough cash with him to leave behind for her expenses. Nawin said that he would arrange for it and not let her feel that she was still a burden on her parents. Aarti was relieved to hear that.

Aarti wanted to drop her studies and focus on rearing their son. She did not want to stay at her parents' house when she had a baby of her own. Nawin discovered that the financial condition of her parents was not as good as his father Dev thought before he arranged his marriage.

In fact, there was almost no dowry in that marriage. People suggested that for being in very dire financial conditions Aarti's parents married their daughter to a man from Nepal, as suitable Indian grooms demanded a heavy dowry.

It was a trend in the border areas that the Indian people were ready to marry off their daughters to a suitable Nepali groom but they seldom accepted a bride from the Nepalese side, where dowry was still not in practice as in India. So the difference between cultures of the two nations was emerging.

Nawin felt that marriages were the same everywhere, whether in Kathmandu or in his native place. People lied and misrepresented themselves as much as they could.

He felt happy that now he had a son on whom he could focus on. Maybe he will become the man that Nawin tried to become. The world had always been a tremendous agitation to deal with. Nawin always tried to shut the doors to it to keep his cool.

He assured Aarti that he would soon find a suitable living place for them and then take her and Rahul to Kathmandu. He was thinking of changing jobs and so many other things. But life in Kathmandu was in turmoil to raise a family. There were no favourable conditions for doing a job or business either. He wished in his heart that Aarti remained with her parents for the present. He was thinking of sending her enough money to take care of her expenses every month.

She was unwilling to live with Dev and Nisha and Dinesh at Nawin's home. She found that Dev was too old to take care of his grandson and besides he was preoccupied with Dinesh to pay attention to anyone else. She informed Nawin that Nisha and his father were looking for a girl to marry Dinesh for some time. They thought that he was normal to have a wife and children. Nawin ironically smiled on hearing it.

A short time after the SAARC conference, a few senior politicians from India met in Nepal, at the residence of Nepali Congress leader Ganesh Man Singh. He was declared leader of the planned joint movement of all parties against the king. The Indian leaders addressed the people, exhorting them to do away with the rule of the rule of the king. Things were really bad in Nepal, and the revolution started as soon those Indian leaders gave a voice to the sentiments felt by the Nepalese people. The audio recording of those speeches, in Hindi, were widely circulated, even though they were promptly banned by the government.

A friend of Nawin brought one of the audio cassettes to his apartment. On the way he was accosted by a police-officer, who turned out to be Nawin's cousin. He let Nawin's friend go, even though he knew that the man was going to Nawin's apartment with the banned cassette. Over drinks they listened to it while discussing how kind the cousin had been. There was a general uncertainty among the people about the future. Nawin and his friend were not all that anxious, for they did not have too much to lose, no matter whatever happened. Similar was the case with the large majority of people.

Chandrasekhar, who was to become the Indian PM in the days ahead, and S.M. Swami, who was a teacher of King Birendra at Harvard university, among others, made a clarion call in Hindi to do away with the monarchy in Nepal, to a cheering Nepalese crowd. The revolution had started, though the Indian leaders returned the next day. Everyday there were mass gatherings, amidst the news of arrests of the people leading the uprising.

One day the police opened fire on a crowd gathered at Tundikhel, the open fields in the centre of the city. Nawin, on the roof of his apartment building, along with other tenants, counted fourteen gun-shots. Nine people died in that first firing and a few others were injured. They were admitted to Bir Hospital, across the road.

Shootings became routine.

Nawin heard that a girl, who was looking out of the window of her house at a procession was shot dead by the police, in Patan, the ancient city across the river. Ill-equipped, the Nepali police used weapons which were primitive. 303 were their most advanced rifles. Their guns injured more people than they killed. Also, they did not have enough protective gear and the pelting of stones or petrol bombs thrown at them by the mobs injured many policemen. A large number of protestors proceeded towards the royal palace, one day. Finding army soldiers ready with machine guns in firing position in front of it, they went towards the road where there were many college buildings. Things seemed to escalate by the day.

The palace was empty, however. The king was in Pokhra for his yearly visit which lasted more than two months. Pokhra was the headquarters of one of the five developmental regions of the country, and the king visited them by turns, making the headquarters his base. It was rumoured that during one such formal visit to the Far-West developmental region a few years back, officials purchased cauliflowers from the market and planted them in the fields, to show the king how well the agriculture was flourishing there. Everyone but the king seemed aware of that charade.

It was not a surprise that things were getting worse, in spite of the king's yearly visits to the different developmental regions. By being lodged stubbornly in Pokhra, he tried to pretend everything was normal. But things were deteriorating fast in Kathmandu. The protestors attacked the statue of late King Mahendra, the father of the ruling king, in front of the palace, a few days later. The police opened fire and hundreds of people were killed, as per unconfirmed reports. Reports of protests, detentions and deaths came from all the major towns of the country.

Almost every week, there was a black-out in the evening, in Kathmandu. People switched off all the lights of their houses, then clapped or hooted from their roofs in the darkness. It was in support of the revolution. Houses, which failed to switch off the lights at a given time, were pelted with stones from the darkness.

Sometime later, it was rumoured that the king was willing to talk with the leaders of the revolution, but his queen and other members of the royal family were holding him back. By this time professionals like doctors, engineers and pilots had joined the popular movement against the king, through their organisations.

Also, it was reported, by the private newspapers publishing illegally, that the king had been offered a new treaty by the Indian government, in which there were proposals to reduce Nepal to the vassal status similar to Bhutan. In exchange, India would help the king crush the revolution. But, wisely, further reports maintained, the king became prepared finally, to accept the demands of his own subjects, rather than the dictates of a foreign country. By now nearly a thousand people had lost their lives, in the revolution.

The world itself was in turmoil. Around this time, the Berlin wall was torn down, and the USSR was about to disintegrate, eventually into fourteen countries. 'Glasnost' and 'perestroika', the Russian words for openness and reforms, coined by the Russian leader Gorbachev, who overlooked the change into a democracy, were the words most often appearing in the newspapers world over.

The Tiananmen Square students protest had been brutally crushed by the army in China. There was political instability in India too. Elections were on the cards once again, as the coalition cobbled together by V.P. Singh was coming apart. The Indian army had entered Sri Lanka earlier, when Rajiv Gandhi was the PM, to crush the Tamil uprising there. The revolutionaries there wanted a separate country. It was rumoured that their leader, Prabhakaran, lived for some time in Nepal. He held talks with the Sri Lankan President Jaywardhane in Bhutan, and then went to Sri Lanka, to lead a civil war. That war was turning bloodier everyday.

Jaywardhane was to be killed in a bomb-blast by separatist Tamil guerrillas a few years later, for having invited the Indian army to crush their war. The Indian army itself suffered heavy casualties. Finally it was withdrawn by V.P. Singh, towards the end of his nearly two years in power.

About a hundred thousand people of Nepalese ethnicity had been evicted from Bhutan. The government declared them foreigners in a country which claimed to be a Buddhist theocracy. They had been living there for centuries. More of them were to arrive in eastern Nepal in the following years. Bhutan was ruled by a king who had married four sisters at a time. He was to ban smoking in the country when he himself stopped smoking, many years later.

The Nepalese King, still the absolute ruler, ordered the arrest of Teknath Rijal. Rijal had held responsible positions in the Bhutanese government before things turned bad for him and other people of Nepalese ethnicity in Bhutan. He managed to flee to Nepal with his family, but was handed over to the Bhutanese government.

He was subjected to great physical and mental torture and remained in prison for almost a decade. His crime was peacefully struggling for the rights of Bhutanese people of Nepalese ethnicity.

Some equated his struggle with that of Nelson Mandela in South Africa. Mandela was freed around this time, after twenty-six years in prison. He became the President of his country for two terms, after the apartheid regime was finally done away with. It was many years later, when democracy had been established in Nepal, that Teknath Rijal was released and returned to Nepal, on the initiative of some international human rights organisations. He later wrote his biography, in which he dealt in detail with the inhumane treatment to which he and other people of Nepalese ethnicity were subjected by the Royal Bhutanese government.

The Bhutanese King persistently declined diplomatic relations with China, its only other neighbour, like Nepal. China was to soon emerge as a major world power during the years to come. Its taking over of Hong Kong from a reluctant Britain was an acknowledgement of Chinese arrival as a world power. Bhutan had diplomatic relations with only three countries in the world.

Terms like 'Gross National Happiness', coined by the Bhutanese King, as an alternative to Gross National Production, received approval of Britain and other European countries in the UN, in the coming years. That he was responsible for cleansing his nation of Nepalese ethnicity, the world chose to ignore.

These European countries became obsessed with the notion of containing China, which was to become the second largest economy of the world, after the USA, and the largest trade partner of almost every country of the world. China was also to prove most of the Western travel writers wrong by linking Lhasa, the capital of Tibet, to the Chinese railway network. The Chinese building of an all-weather, many thousand kilometres long railway track, over the Tibetan plateau, higher than three thousand metres on average, was considered a unique engineering feat. It was also building the world's largest dams, sea-bridges, thermal and nuclear power plants in the meanwhile.

Bhutanese refugees in Nepal multiplied to two hundred thousand. They were offered the visa to Canada, Australia and the US. However, the US and EU ambassadors threatened to not give such visas to the Nepalese, many years later, who were found to be involved in political agitation in Nepal.

While maintaining a low profile, P.V. Narasimha Rao was able to begin an irreversible process of economic reforms, which to this day pays dividends to India. In the latter part of his rule, he invited the hostility of Sonia Gandhi, the Italian-born widow of Rajiv Gandhi. She had joined active politics, in spite of her initial diffidence.

A large amount of wealth generated was being siphoned out to the safer heavens, as an open economy entailed and facilitated. Narasimha Rao survived his illness to write a nearly thousand page autobiography, in which he described life as no different from politics. An outstanding and attention-riveting remark of his was that 'In India, while being a PM not taking a decision could be a decision in itself.'

The retired Sri Lankan President, Jaywardhane, into his late seventies, who had invited the Indian army to his country to contain the war of the Tamil separatists, was also killed in a bomb-blast in Colombo, sometime during this period. Tamils were proving the most deadly guerrilla fighters the world had seen. Two leaders of the region, who had participated in the SAARC conference in Kathmandu had been killed very violently. But more were destined to meet a similar fate.

They included the King Birendra himself and Benazir Bhutto of Pakistan. The politics of the region was divided into ethnic and communal lines very deeply, notwithstanding the boundaries of the nations. The people who led a nation often paid the price with their lives. Only a few like Narasimha Rao were wise and lucky enough to retire and live a peaceful life to write an autobiography.

By now Nawin had brought Aarti and his son to Kathmandu. He had hired a flat in a location where a few people of his profession lived with their families. So they had built a kind of community where they helped each other in taking care of their families. So being on tour was not a big problem.

Nawin took his family home only once a year now, when Rahul's school was closed for vacations. He left them with Aarti's parents and returned to Kathmandu. He had changed jobs and joined a Nepalese Pharmaceutical company and was making decent money now. He went back to collect Aarti and Rahul a few weeks later, when Rahul's school was about to resume. He was planning to buy a flat and a car soon.

His brother Anil had secured a job in a private company in Delhi and had married a local woman. Her parents had migrated from Nepal and had settled in Delhi. They owned a small business. Anil too had a daughter. Anil and his family came home to see Nisha and Dev often, whose life was preoccupied as usual with taking care of Dinesh.

Nawin was proud of the way Anil had established himself. His mental picture of Anil was that of a small boy with tears in his eyes, holding a banana but not eating it. It was how he looked, the day their mother died.

In his heart Nawin was not very pleased with his condition. He wanted to do something else, achieve something more. The simple life he had earned for himself after a great deal of hardship was not what he had in mind. The adversities were immense to reach where he presently was. But it was never his destination.

He wanted a change. But it was risky now. With a wife and a child to take care of, he was unable to see how he could try something else. These thoughts tormented him and he found himself as adrift as ever.

In such a state of mind, the news from Aarti of her second pregnancy was least welcome. He was practising the use of contraceptives in order to avoid that. Big families always left him feeling crowded. He stayed away from home for a similar reason even when he was young. Men and women, according to him, had better things to do and achieve than merely breeding a brood.

'But how did it happen? We have been trying to avoid it, have we not?' he remarked on hearing the news from Aarti.

'I don't know. You are the one who reads books on that subject and use many things. You should know,' Aarti retorted. She had thought that Nawin would welcome the news as Rahul was three years old and had started to attend school. Nawin thought about the hardships he and Aarti would face in bringing up another child. This time away from his or Aarti's parents. He thought if his wont to take a chance without a condom just after Aarti's period caused it.

'I think we should abort it,' he said decisively.

Aarti was disappointed to hear him say so and rejected Nawin's idea. She wanted to have one more child to complete their family and thought it was the right time to do so. Nawin was afraid of his life becoming crowded. The apartment they were living in was not very big. A new child would mean a lot of additional expenses and a huge drain on their time and energies. But Aarti remained adamant.

Nawin tried to persuade her for the next few days. He told her about his job insecurities at present and the tight financial condition. Aarti finally yielded. But she took a promise from him that they will have another child a few years later and definitely before she tuned thirty. She considered that age as maximum to bear a child for a woman.

Living at Kathmandu, away from their parents, their son Rahul had created a bond between Nawin and Aarti. They depended on each other for they had no one else to fall back on. They had the usual cynicism and antagonism towards each other, which couples in an arranged marriage normally have.

But as the years passed by they found it better to keep that way. The business of making a living consumed all their energies and time to think about anything else. But it surfaced as soon as they visited their parents or someone from the family came to visit them.

They went to the government Maternity Hospital at Thapathali. The attending lady doctor informed them that abortion was not possible as it was illegal except if the mother's life was in danger due to pregnancy.

Nawin tried to argue a little with the doctor, enquiring what a family would do with many children to avoid yet another.

'They should practise the different methods of contraception. You can go to our counselling centre to check about them,' she replied. A middle-aged woman of very slight built and very short height, the doctor was cunningly staring at Nawin and Aarti from behind her thick glasses on a wide-rimmed frame of plastic. There was a male junior doctor who was sitting near them, attending to other patients in a very busy clinic. He inadvertently smiled to hear those words of his senior.

'But we have been using condom and somehow it failed,' Nawin said in a voice choking with emotion.

'You seem an educated man. You should use them properly,' the doctor replied. She added, 'Next.'

Nawin and Aarti left the stools they were sitting on. While they were coming out of the clinic making their way in the crowd, they were approached by an attendant from the clinic.

She was an elderly woman, a widow, as her pale coloured dress and necklace of white fake pearls suggested. In her hands she had the cards of the patients waiting, who she would send inside the clinic when it was their turn .

'Bhai, listen to me. If you want a solution, take a phone number from me. This doctor has a clinic in Putli Sadak. You can get the treatment you want there,' she said in a surreptitious manner.

'You can check the cost over phone. It is not too expensive. We get a lot of people like you here. She is an experienced doctor. Do not go to other people. As at times it is too risky,' she added.

'Take the number from her,' Aarti prompted him. 'We will decide later.'

A few days later Nawin took Aarti to the doctor's clinic on his motorbike, leaving Rahul with a neighbour for a few hours.

The clinic was in the main road of Putli Sadak area on the first floor of a very old building made of wood and mud. They went upstairs through the creaky, narrow stairs. A very dim bulb lit it poorly and there was a risk of slipping and falling over.

There were nearly half a dozen women waiting for their turn in the waiting room. They found the same attendant they met at the Maternity hospital, who gave them the phone number of the private clinic of the doctor. She greeted them with a smile and asked them to wait for their turn. She told them that the doctor had already performed a few cases and one was going on inside the clinic.

When their turn came Nawin and Aarti entered the clinic. They found that a woman was lying on the sofa and another was resting on the operating table. There was a nurse who was assisting the doctor. While they talked to the doctor, the doctor called the man who came with the patient who was lying on the sofa and asked him to take the patient outside and let her rest in the waiting room with some hot drink. If she felt comfortable they could go home – the doctor instructed. She asked the nurse to shift the other patient from the operating table to the sofa and asked Aarti to go and undress before lying on the operating table. She asked Nawin to pay the cost of the operation.

It was surprisingly simple. But the cost was higher than what Nawin had thought. While they waited afterwards in the waiting room, drinking the coffee Nawin had purchased in plastic glasses from outside, Aarti said that she felt fine and was ready to go home. There was some embarrassment about the operation so they didn't talk much.

But once they were home with Rahul, Aarti said that she liked very much the sari that the doctor was wearing and wanted one of the same colour and quality. Nawin was surprised at how easily she had regained normalcy. He, however, told her that the doctor made a lot of money every day to afford that kind of sari. He would have to check the cost, before he decided to buy her one.

He was unhappy that abortion was illegal and had to be purchased after paying such a high cost. He thought about the overcrowded homes in villages in the distant locations he had seen. And the consequences.

Abortion should have been made legal like in India long ago, he thought. But the system ruling Nepal was impervious to the many needs of the people it ruled.

IN Kathmandu, things were far from being settled. Immediately, after the King accepted the multiparty democratic system, he swore in Krishna Bhattarai as the new interim prime minister. The appointment was on the recommendation of the leader of revolution Ganesh Man Singh, who declined to accept the post, offered by the king. The last decade of the century had begun.

The police force, still wearing khaki-dress, revolted against the democratic government. Somehow the police were controlled during the next few days. But then another police force, dressed in black, appeared. It was backed by the members of the royal family, it was assumed. The police in black dress tried to create an atmosphere of terror in the society, by engaging in petty gang-fights or robberies in the narrow streets of the capital, in the evenings. The efforts to begin a counter revolution, to undermine the democracy, were working. The new Constitution, which was meant to be a document of compromise between the king, the democratic forces and the leftists, was still being drafted.

To prevent the police in black dress from undermining the society, local youths organised and kept vigil in their own streets with sharp metal weapons and torch-lights, till late into the night. There also surfaced rumours that the drinking water supply was poisoned by anti-social elements. But they all proved mere rumours.

People gradually decided how to handle the police dressed in black. Over the next few days many of those men were pummelled or stoned to death, by local people in different areas of the city. In Kalimati, one morning, people got hold of about a dozen of them - all dressed in black - and beat them with sticks and iron rods. The men became badly wounded in a few minutes.

Then they were tied with ropes to a hand driven cart used to carry goods in the narrow streets of the city. Small fire-arms and sharp knives recovered from them were tied together by a rope to make a garland, hung on the front of the cart. Some of them were dead, others were breathing their last. It was a bright and hot summer day. People came as a mob, pushing the cart in front of them, from Kalimati to the exhibition road, displaying their rods and sticks. As soon they crossed the Mahendra Police Club building, two trucks full of men came, and took possession of the cart by force. They hurled the bodies into the trucks and took them to the traffic police office at Singh Durbar.

After this incident, those men dressed in black ceased to appear in the streets at dusk. But anger against the police - even dressed in Khaki - had not abated. A senior police officer lost his eye while he was trying to disperse a crowd gathered near the University area of Kirtipur.

Girija Koirala became the elected PM, after the interim PM Krishna Bhattarai successfully drafted a new constitution and held the general elections, during a period nearly a year long and under a continuous threat of counter-revolution by the royalists. The king still controlled the army and was the head of the state, as per the new Constitution. But people had the rights to elect their own government. In the elections however, surprisingly Krishna Bhattarai lost badly from a constituency in Kathmandu. It was speculated that his political rival Girija Koirala manipulated things to cause his defeat. The leader of the popular uprising, Ganesh Man Singh, himself did not stand as a candidate. He instead proposed his son and his wife as candidates. His wife lost the election, while his son won. It made Girija Koirala more powerful within the Congress party.

It was an uncomfortable arrangement: to have a king as the head of the state in a democracy where the elected leaders were so much divided. Meanwhile, the communist parties were unionising the civil servants against the government. Every week there was a strike going on against the government by civil servants. At times it became violent and a curfew had to be imposed.

It appeared a new revolution was brewing within an year or two of the previous one.

Weather came to the rescue of Koirala. It rained very heavily that summer. Many of the bridges linking Kathmandu to the rest of Nepal were washed away. There was a huge loss of life and property due to landslides and floods all over the country. 'Bailey-bridges' arrived from countries like Britain and the USA at the International airport at Kathmandu, and it was several weeks before Kathmandu was once again linked by roads to other towns.

These events momentarily distracted the communist led protests against the Koirala government. The crisis seemed to deepen, however, as the protests resumed after the monsoons.

The Girija Government sold off most of the factories built by the Chinese government in Nepal at throw-away prices, to crony businessmen of the Congress Party. The reason for the sales was that the factories were loss-making and hence not sustainable in the era of privatisation and market economy. It also disposed of two Boeing 737 aircrafts of the state-owned Royal Nepal Airlines corporation, at scrap metal price. The planes had flown to Germany, for maintenance. Those aircrafts were still in service even a decade later, owned by an African company.

The politicians' need for money to run for elections was becoming obvious. Selling or purchasing government-owned properties was the easiest way to muster that. The opposition parties intensified the protests when they learned about the designs of the politicians in power.

The government also handed over the management of state-owned banks to foreign consultants, after a foreign private auditing company named KPMG declared them 'technically-insolvent.'

By now the banks were plagued with bad loans, often to the cronies of the government. Thatcherism, in practice and apparently successful in Britain, was being aped by the barely literate politicians in India or Nepal. It served them well by making them and their cronies rich. Also, the Westminster model of democracy imitated from Britain ensured that politics turned a family occupation of a selected few.

The Girija government, also, remarkably, broke the tradition of receiving a few hundred sheep as Dashain gift from the Chinese government. If it was an assertion of the self-esteem of the Nepalese people, who lived in a democratic country now, it totally lacked while dealing with any other country except China. China also had started to increasingly complain about the 'Free-Tibet' activities taking place in Nepal.

In the meanwhile, a mid-term election took place due to the internal struggle for power within the Congress Party. It brought into the office a moderate communist leader Manmohan Adhikary, as PM of a minority government. He, remarkably, raised the issue of abolishing the 'unequal' treaties between India and Nepal, while on a visit to India.

But his government lasted for less than a year. Manmohan Adhikary, surviving a helicopter crash-landing near Nepalganj, from where he was returning after taking part in a ceremony, resigned from his bed at Tribhuwan University Teaching Hospital, where his broken back was being treated, after he was about to lose a vote of confidence in the House of Representatives. He read his resignation from his bed, telecast live by the Nepal television; watched also by the House of Representatives, which was waiting to elect a new PM.

Deuba became the new Congress PM, with the support of Koirala, who had been considered his mentor until then. Their relations were to sour in the days ahead. Deuba had a strong political base in the west of the country and was ambitious too, unlike the hitherto main rival of Girija, Krishna Bhattarai. Bhattarai had the image of being a saint and had never won an election. He lived with his many mistresses, and contested on prompting that he was not a saint at all. But he was unmarried.

While these developments were taking place, a group of communists, having some representatives in the House of Representatives, declared themselves Maoists and presented a forty point demand to PM Deuba. Deuba could not fulfil those demands, as they were mostly against the country's submissive policies about India. The Maoists then declared a war against the state and its leadership went underground. Maoist fighters started attacking the police outposts in the rural parts of the country, running away with the captured weapons after killing the officers on duty.

This new uprising seemed to be gaining ground in the rural parts of the country, by the day. 'A stitch in time saves nine,' said a headline of the English daily, *The Kathmandu Post*, urging the government to heed to the demands of the Maoists. But it was not to be.

In Kathmandu, Prince Paras was involved in accidents frequently. He once killed a famous folk singer near the royal palace, running over him in the Pajero jeep he so often drove, as did the other royals. He once threatened a police officer by showing him an automatic weapon at Patan Dhoka, because the officer had the temerity to stop his speeding car covered with black glass. The police officer saluted in panic, it was heard. In another instance he was found with a similar weapon with him, driving fast in a Pajero near the royal palace. Once he hit an electricity pole with his vehicle, injuring himself a little, at Maitighar.

A low ranking police officer declined to identify him, when he broke a traffic rule in his Pajero, and arrested him. But the Prince was saluted as soon he was taken to the Police Headquarters. These reports did not help the new liberal image of royalty, which the king was trying to build and project. The crown prince was approaching the age of thirty and had not married yet. He was considered the most eligible bachelor at that time, among the families who had marital relationships with the royal family.

It was speculated in Kathmandu mostly, where the people had the time and interest to always gossip about the activities of the royal family, as a part of their social discussions, that other princes were not getting a suitable bride to marry. Every aristocrat wanted his or her daughter to be the next queen, instead of the wife of a lesser prince.

Prince Paras, the only son of the younger brother of the King, Gyanendra, eventually married a girl from a migrant royal family of India. His bride lived in Nepal, with her widowed mother, after her father died early. Her mother possibly shifted to Nepal fearing the threat ensued after the death of her husband due to the property dispute in the family.

Earlier, during an electoral violence in India, a former king had been murdered. It was the election which brought Indira Gandhi to power for the first time, with the symbol of a cow-feeding-the-calf on a tri-colour Indian congress flag. The symbol later changed to an open palm.

The royal families of yore in India were facing tough time after the independence; and more so after Indira Gandhi scrapped their remaining privileges. For them having marital relations with the Nepalese royal family was a cherished ambition. For the royalty in Nepal retained all the power and glamour which they had been denied in the Indian republic. Some of them had joined the electoral politics of India and made a distinct place for themselves.

During this time, the only daughter of the king, Princess Shruti, married the grandson of Kaisher Rana. Kaisher was the Rana aristocrat who established the Kaisher library and then donated it for public use.

In the meanwhile, another midterm election took place. Krishna Bhattarai became the new PM, this time an elected one. Koirala, in spite of their rivalry, had proposed him as the candidate for PM in the elections, on account of his clean image. Koirala himself had been accused of involvement in several corruption cases. Soon after being sworn-in, Krishna Bhattarai declared that the army will take care of the Maoists if they do not join the mainstream.

That did not last long.

Koirala ousted him before long by manoeuvring shrewdly. Suddenly Koirala was the PM again. It was throughout suspected that the royals were supporting the Maoists, who were now operating from India. The Girija-led government was unable to do much in such circumstances. The king once was reported to have asked the government to find out who the Maoists were. Police moral was plummeting by the Maoist attacks, in which they ransacked the police post almost invariably, and killed the officers even after they surrendered. Koirala's plan to crush the Maoists by using the police in operations such as 'kilo-shera-two' had started to attract a fierce comeuppance of the Maoists.

Police were nearly confined to the district headquarters only, across the country, leaving the area beyond for the Maoists to carry out their campaign of extortion, torture and murder. The government built a better armed police force, when the first round of discussing a ceasefire with Maoists failed and the conflict escalated. Officers in the regular police force started to desert it in significant numbers.

The situation appeared getting out of hand with every passing week. Newspapers published photographs of ransacked police posts with the mutilated bodies of the policemen spread around; and the stories about Maoists' torture of surrendering cops before murder. Girija Koirala asked the king to mobilise the army against the Maoists. The king declined. He said he cannot use the Royal Nepalese Army against his own people.

But then the Maoists attacked and ransacked a district military barrack at Dang. They killed most of the troops including the commanding officer. This time they took away the artillery pieces also. As politicians bickered, and the king watched the spectacle with interest, the Maoists gained an enormous ground outside it.

ONE morning Nawin got a call: Dev had died the previous evening. He was happy that this news did not catch him battling hangover yet another morning. The pressures of city life and his job were stressful and he had taken to the drinking habit, consuming alcohol almost every evening.

In fact he had avoided drinking the previous evening, though he was attending a party. He was in his gloomy phase, which left him sober on those rare evenings, when he avoided alcohol. This phase lasted several days at times. During this time he could clearly see how helpless he was, to have been where he was. He thought he was in control mostly. But often he was surprised. But not this time.

His father had suffered heart problems for some time. A lifelong smoker, he coughed very badly during the night, when Nawin was young. It disturbed his sleep, making him worried if his father was seriously sick. To this day, the persistent cough of his wife or son, due to the allergies they suffered when the season changed, made Nawin anxious.

It was only after he had completed the age of sixty that Dev gave up smoking, as his body could not take it anymore. He coughed no more during the night. By then, however, his chest had turned barrel-shaped and the doctor had warned of a heart-attack. Now it had finally happened.

Nawin went home. Anil was already mourning along with Dinesh and their step-mother, Nisha. The neighbours extolled the life of Dev, noting he never got involved in any dispute or controversy. Nawin's only surviving uncle too lived with them during the mourning period. He smoked hashish often but was a talkative and humorous person. His company made the time less gloomy.

Nisha cooked for Dinesh, Anil, Nawin and herself the only meal of the day they were supposed to take during the mourning period, which was boiled rice with sugar and ghee. They did not take even salt during those thirteen days. Their uncle however, though mourning, was free to prepare for himself only, separately, regular meals but no meat. After smoking his hashish cigarettes, he sang old movie songs while he cooked for himself a tasty meal, as the sweet smell of onions and spices frying noisily on the stove betrayed. It kindled Nawin's appetite. He wanted to have regular meals as soon as possible. But during mourning it was not allowed.

The uncle ate heartily and noisily, in another room, hungry due to the hashish he smoked. He said it was what he always did at home, like many of his fellow villagers: Prepare meals as the only domestic duty, high on hashish, apart from bringing water from a spring in the morning. It was the wives of the villagers, who were clear-headed to work in the fields and maintain the livestock. They also brought firewood from the pine jungle amidst which the temple was situated.

Everyone, especially Nisha, worried about what would happen to Dinesh. Dinesh did not understand death. He did not even cry on the death of a person who, after he was born, dedicated most of his time and energies on trying to improve his physical health and learning capacities, never losing the hope that somehow Dinesh could be like his step-brothers. But it was not to be. On the mental level Dinesh remained a three year old with a limited capacity of speech, though his physical age was twenty-five.

Nawin recalled that only six months back he had visited his father after a gap of three years. He was a little sick. Nawin took him to a cardiologist in the town Sora, where his father used to take him and his mother and Anil, during his childhood, to draw his pension. The cardiologist made some changes in the medicines he was taking and told that the condition of his heart would be stable with them.

Dev, now seventy-eight, was very happy to see him. He wished that Nawin stayed back a little more. He said he was so happy to have lived a life with its pleasures and tragedies. He also said that he was the second most aged person in the town and living to that age was a reward by itself. But as usual, the concern for Dinesh surfaced during discussions and he wanted an assurance from Nawin that he would take care of his step-brother. Nawin assured his father as best as he could, before he returned to his job and family in Kathmandu.

Now the day was here.

After completing the thirteen days of mourning Anil had returned to Delhi. He told Nawin that he was looking for a job in Dubai, where the salaries were much higher. But the brokers who arranged such jobs were often not very reliable. He said that his in-laws were ready to look after his family for a few years after he went abroad. His ambition was to make enough money within a few years and then live a life of comfort.

Nawin was happy to learn about his plans. He was proud how well his younger brother had shaped up into a fine and responsible man.

He lingered at home after Anil left. He had a few more duties to do. He also wanted to mourn a little more the death of his father. Also he thought about how Nisha and Dinesh would do without Dev around now.

Nawin took his step-mother to various offices at Sora, along with Dinesh, arranging for her to receive the pension of Dev. Nisha was seventy, and was not literate. Nawin then returned to Kathmandu, thinking that, somehow, they will be fine. After all they were mother and son.

There were no financial worries for them and they had a home. Looking after Dinesh would be a big burden for Nisha, Nawin knew. But he could do nothing about it. At times he thought that only if Nisha had not become pregnant, at that late age, their lives might have been very different.

But things happened over which one had no control. They just had to live with it, and try to minimise the damage. He returned to Kathmandu, promising Nisha that he would come back at the earliest to take care of them.

A few months later Aarti was pregnant again. This time Nawin didn't think about an abortion. They were ready for a second child.

She was a little worried about Rahul though. She was not sure how they will be able to handle her delivery and the child. They consulted a few neighbours. They were given various types of advice.

When it was time for the delivery, and Aarti had developed labour pains, Nawin asked a neighbour to look after Rahul after he returned from school. His wife offered to accompany them to the hospital, since men were not allowed inside the labour room. Nawin accepted thankfully, wishing in his heart that he could reciprocate in some manner this crucial help.

They took a taxi. The same evening Aarti gave birth to a healthy baby boy. It was surprisingly easier than her first delivery, she told Nawin.

Next day in the afternoon they all returned home. Rahul was very anxious to see them, though Nawin had talked to him several times over the phone. He was very happy and curious to see his brother.

The neighbour had arranged for a woman to take care of the mother and the newly born - washing them, giving them a massage, etc. Her charges were high but her services indispensable, at least during the first few months, particularly to people like Nawin and Aarti, who had no relations in the city to help. Nawin was once again indebted to his neighbour, an elderly man who had a son working in Australia and a daughter who attended college in Kathmandu. He worked in a bank and was near his retirement age. He told Nawin that he too had brought up his family in Kathmandu alone, without relations to help.

Aarti rested for the first few weeks, leaving her bed only to walk a little as suggested by the doctor. The stitches had to heal properly and without catching an infection.

Aarti and her younger son flourished well during this time. Nawin's worries about the matters after the arrival of a second child were forgotten.

Rahul liked to talk to his brother for hours. Nawin felt happy at these developments. He thought he would work even harder to secure a better living for his family. After three months they discontinued the services of the servant, as Aarti felt good enough to carry on like before.

Their neighbour and his wife guided them well whenever they sought their help. Nawin thought he would do whatever he could to reciprocate their help.

Nepal

Maoist War and the Royal Massacre

ON the first day of June, 2001, very early in the morning, while still in bed, Nawin heard the phone ring. His boss was on line. He told Nawin that firing had taken place in the royal palace and the King was feared to have been assassinated. He looked at the clock on the wall, it was still a few minutes short of five. Nawin was not sure what he should say. His boss asked him to follow the news on television.

It was Saturday, a weekly holiday. He had returned late from his job last evening, as on the last day of the month he had to work late to close the sales. His office was on Durbar Marg, only about one hundred meters away from the royal palace. He had heard no sounds of firing or gunshots before he left office at around 10:00 pm.

Nawin switched on the television and found the same news being reported on the BBC and CNN news channels, along with the Indian news channels. Nepal TV started its telecast by 6:00 am. There were devotional songs playing, sung by a few male and female devotees, in a temple, adorned in their finery dancing to the beat. It was a crude dance and had no rhythm or method.

Nawin tuned in the FM radio. A few channels reported the news. Early on, there was confusion, in the things being reported on all the channels on TV or radio. Finally, the state-owned TV reported the death of the king and almost all of the immediate family. '...When an automatic weapon fired itself,' it offered, as an explanation.

It also reported that the Crown Prince, also injured in the incident, was in a serious condition at the military hospital at Chhawani.

The government declared seven-days' mourning and suspension of all scheduled programmes on Nepal TV and Radio Nepal. This announcement was followed by mourning music which was to continue for the next week, interrupted only by news bulletins. The sad sound of a solitary cord from a sitar filled Nawin's apartment, and made things gloomier and more confusing, as the hours passed, with no plausible explanation of what had actually happened or how.

Restlessness could be felt in the air as the day progressed. Everybody wanted to know more than what was being reported.

Thankfully,.continuous updates continued to be reported on the foreign TV and radio channels. They were digging more into the present and past of Nepal, interviewing ordinary people and the people related to the royal family, trying to find out what had really happened. Had it been only a decade back, people might not have heard anything more than what the state-owned media reported, between the mourning music it was playing. But this was the age of cell phones and the Internet. Pressure was building upon the authorities to come up with something better than the first explanation, that '... the automatic weapon fired itself.'

By afternoon, Nepal TV showed the bodies of the entire royal family, including the married daughter of the king, his youngest brother Dhirendra, and his younger son Nirajan. The corpses were placed on the ground outside the military hospital. The lawn they were laid on was sparse, the red clay having very little grass. Hindu death-rituals demanded a dead body, even if it was that of the king, to be immediately removed from the cot or bed and laid on the ground. But the dead royals could have perhaps been put on stretchers instead of the bare ground.

The bodies were covered with a sheet, only their faces were showing. The face of the queen had a mask on it, perhaps because it had been disfigured by shooting. Close-up footage on Nepal TV showed a few flies on the face of the dead king. His mouth was open, his high front-teeth showing. He had been the most powerful man in Nepal, and also popular more recently, having built up an image of a liberal king.

One of the king's sisters and her husband too was reported dead. (Later that day, the mother of the deceased brother-in-law of the king too was reported to have died of a heart attack.) His entire immediate family had been massacred inside his own palace, despite being guarded by nearly five-thousand soldiers directly under his command. The Royal Guards were separately recruited and trained from the regular army. They were treated like an elite force, under a separate General, who reported directly to the king. (The daughter of Vivek Shah, the In-office General in the Royal Palace, and a relation to the royals, was said to be one of the choices for the marriage of the Crown-prince.)

The shooting killed the family members of the king while they were having a week-end dinner party with the royal family and their closest relations. So, amongst the people and in the place he considered himself safest, except for his two infant grand-daughters, from his daughter, who were also present there, none else survived from the immediate family of King Birendra. A grandson could have been his legal heir but not a granddaughter.

Heads of different government bodies, including the PM Girija Koirala, the chiefs of the security services, senior officials and close friends of the royal family all paid their respects to the departed souls, spread on the ground on the patchy lawn of the Army hospital. That evening the bodies were cremated at the crematorium near Pashupatinath temple. They were taken directly from the grounds of the military hospital, as the Hindu religion suggests the earliest cremation possible.

Nawin saw the sad scene telecast live by Nepal TV that evening. Nearly a dozen bodies belonging to the royal family burned on the funeral pyres. When those bodies were being taken to the Pashupatinath, on the shoulders of Army men, a large crowd gathered on the way. People came from places all over, walking long distances, to pay their last respects to their king.

Mourning music on Radio Nepal or Nepal TV continued, apart from the bulletins or live-telecasts. Meanwhile, the BBC and the CNN tried ever harder to uncover what had happened - but without much success. People, including government employees, shaved their heads in droves. They were mourning the death of their king, following the tradition in the country. It was reported a few days later that Girija Koirala, the PM, also shaved his head, after a little reluctance. But the leaders of the communist parties did not do so, as was reported by the local newspapers.

By the time it was dark, people were seen returning on foot to their villages in the outskirts of Kathmandu. They had walked miles in the morning to stand on the route through which the funeral procession was to pass, which the official media announced so often - to pay their tribute to late King Birendra, with flowers in their hands. They had to walk because public transport did not operate that day. Rituals were being devised by the people, in response to something which was enormously tragic and needed a deeper enquiry; which seemed to be outside the grasp of the culture, as it had always been.

The next day, an atmosphere of confusion continued.

'The traditional monarchy in Nepal has ended,' declared a senior Maoist leader Babu Ram Bhattarai. He was underground somewhere in India. His declaration was in an article he published in Kantipur, a popular vernacular daily. He suspected that Indian and US intelligence agencies were behind the massacre. He also accepted in the same article, that the Maoists had some working understanding with King Birendra, through his youngest brother Dhirendra.

It was a confirmation of something everybody suspected, for the liberal image of the king was as unconvincing as were the demands of the Maoists to oust a constitutional monarchy. The communists and the king being hand-in-gloves against a democracy trying to take root seemed strange but was entirely natural. One of them had lost power and the other was hoping to make Nepal a communist republic.

It was the age of Internet and e-mail. People had ceased to depend on the government news media for information. For publishing the article of Babu Ram, the government led by Girija Koirala immediately arrested the editor and the publisher of *Kantipur*. They were to be released only after a few days.

'The king is dead, long live the king,' protested a headline in another newspaper. Barbers reduced the cost of head-shaving to a quarter, compelled by the people, as more and more of them were coming out to shave their heads. There was confusion on every face in the street about what had happened and what was in store. Rumours of every kind were rife, suggesting the conspiracy theories and the like.

Nawin went for a long walk the next morning, getting wet by the sporadic drizzle and not caring. There were few vehicles on the road and it appeared as if everything had come to a standstill. He saw barbers shaving the heads under a tree or on a footpath. He joined the crowd, returning home with his shaved head. It was politically correct, he assumed, under the circumstances. He had shaved his head only a few months back, to undertake religious rituals marking the first anniversary of his father's death.

By now Kathmandu was full of reporters from across the world. Each one of them was trying to find out what really had happened and how. But there was no plausible explanation. The surviving members of that incident of the royal family were not available for comment. They included the son-in-law of the late king and the wife of his younger brother Gyanendra, who were reportedly receiving treatment at the military hospital.

The people repeated what the official media had reported, that the Crown Prince massacred his entire family with an automatic weapon, and then shot himself in his head with a pistol, a little distance away from the hall, where the party was taking place. His motive was, as was suggested by the official media of the government, that he was unhappy because his mother refused to allow him to marry a girl of his own choice. For the official media, it was eventually a vast improvement on what it initially reported: '... an automatic weapon fired itself.'

But for most people, that was not enough. It was however, the only theory reported by almost every news channel from around the world. Those reports included interviews with people who had gathered near the royal palace to pay tribute to the large pictures of the slain royals, kept there the next day. A few people, including a beautiful young girl, were pictured shedding tears, which was splashed on the Internet. Some of the people interviewed lamented that the king's death left them orphaned.

Foreign news channels compared the tragedy in Nepal to the massacre of Russian Czar and his family by the Bolsheviks. Doubts were expressed by everyone if the facts would ever be known, as with most other major political assassinations in the world.

Nawin recalled that, sometime ago, he had an opportunity to have a look at the king up close, while he was at the Durbar

Marg, the open, wide road in front of the royal palace. The south gate of the palace suddenly opened, and the entourage of the king came out, with the king himself riding a horse-driven carriage. There was a similar empty carriage ahead of him. He was going to receive the President of Mongolia at the airport. Guards rode the adorned horses before and after him in their impressive colourful headgears and uniforms. It looked stylish.

The Mongolian President was visiting Nepal on his invitation. The king seemed, in his civilian national-dress and Bhadgaunle cap, to have lost an enormous amount of weight. He recently had survived a heart-attack. He then received a cardiac surgery in Britain, sometime later. His guests were no more the head of the states of the European countries. He looked cheerful, nodding his head to the people on either side of the road with his shy smile and his hands folded in greeting. He looked charming.

Nawin also remembered seeing the king driving on the way to the home of one of his sisters, at Kamaladi, a few hundred metres away from the royal palace, near his office. It was a *bhai-tika* day, when a brother visits his sister after the Dipavali festival. As Nawin was about to cross the road, he stopped, seeing a car approaching. Then he saw the king driving. He was driving a shining BMW. He joined his hands to greet him. The king replied by nodding his head and smiling. The queen was on the seat behind.

Lately, the King had started to appear in public informally, which had made him more popular. On one occasion, he was pictured with the queen, walking to the home of his daughter at Kaisher Mahal, just across the road from the western gate of the royal palace. The king was also building closer relations with countries like Mongolia, apart from China, which were not in the list of preferred countries before. Both India and China courted him, making him a chief guest of their state celebrations. Western countries also sought closer ties, conferring on him honorary degrees from their renowned Universities. In spite of the bloody Maoist war raging in the country, the king appeared to be becoming more popular, both at home and abroad.

Nawin remembered when he was about ten years old that the king and queen had come to visit Baitadi. He and a few of his friends went just to look at them, skipping school that day. They started late and walked for two hours uphill. By the time they reached Baitadi, to their utter disappointment they were told that the royal couple had already left.

Since they were there, they took a round of the town, to see the preparation made for welcoming the king. At one place they found oranges arranged on a board to read *Swagatam* or Welcome, from which a few oranges had disappeared. Finding the young boys returning in dejection, an official gave them each small round badges with pictures of the King and the Queen. It was the same badge that most of the officials wore on their chests, with a safety pin on the back of the badge. That memento remained with Nawin for a long time. Anil pestered him for it. When Nawin finally gave it to him, Anil lost it in no time.

Nawin also had the memory of the day of the king's coronation. A female dancer presented fabulous dances on a well adorned stage to the folk-tunes of their area, while big posters of the coloured pictures of the royal couple were garlanded on the stage. A large number of people gathered there to watch the programme, which was glamorous for a small town. The government officials of Nepal present handsomely tipped the dancer.

But it was all over now. The king was dead.

NEXT morning, the unconscious Crown Prince, Dipendra, too was declared dead. He had been declared a king by the Rajparishad, the advisory body to the king with discretionary power in such circumstances, the previous day. The only surviving brother of the king, Gyanendra, who mysteriously was in Pokhra on that fateful Friday evening, who had been earlier declared the regent of the unconscious new king, was declared the new king by the Rajparishad. Dipendra was cremated that evening, which the state-owned TV telecast live.

The new king ascended the throne in Hanumandhoka, the old royal palace. He received Daam, a coin at his feet, and a salute from the security officials; and a bowing of heads with hands folded from the chiefs of the different civilian bodies of the government. The precious crown, with valuable stones of blue or green, adorned his shaven head.

While Army men guarded the way on both sides, facing the other way, the new king rode sitting in his horse-driven carriage, the General of the Army standing beside him, through the New Road and Rani Pokhari road. None in the crowd standing on both sides of the road seemed to cheer the arrival of a new king. Perhaps the army men keeping watch with their automatic rifles on the ready were the reason for the silence; perhaps it was the recent tragedy.

The king entered the Narayanhiti Royal Palace, where just two days back, the massacre which was to haunt the psyche of the

Nepalese people for a long time to come, had taken place. Several years later Nawin was surprised to find the footage of the aftermath of the royal massacre, on You Tube. There were several clips. One clip had an interview of the woman Dipendra wanted to marry. She appeared very harassed. Nawin was surprised to read some of the comments of the pseudonymous viewers, posted on those clips, which offered nothing more than what had already been reported. The comments denounced Hinduism for that incident, and wrote that this was what came in the end, in a Hindu way of life: Self-destruction and pity. Nawin found those comments worthless and distasteful, as they were plainly anti-Hindu more than anything else, for reasons best known to the people who posted them. Indeed, the criminality of the incident needed a more scientific enquiry, instead of the denouncement of a religion.

It could have been mere propaganda, to take attention away from that happening, for none of the comments contested the official explanation of the tragedy. Time was passing by the minute, making the images in the memories of the people blurred, and the rains were washing away the evidence, which could have been important for the forensic purposes.

The change was being felt in Nepal as well. A spiritual guru, preaching on a FM channel in the morning, suggested how people, including the new king, could cope with the tragedy that had taken place in Nepal, in one of his programmes. He was talking as if to the new king specially. He appeared to be one of the savviest in Nepal, who had come to terms with the change in the royal palace before anyone else. In his twisted language, he wanted the new king to appoint him as his spiritual consultant, or something of that sort.

It was after a few months, that one more royal, the wife of Dhirendra, the youngest brother of King Birendra, was to be killed in an accident, when a military helicopter she was boarding came down into the remote Rara Lake. This lake was fabled for its beauty, located at a height of more than three-thousand metres, in the hills in the west. An army doctor on board was the lone survivor in the crash. He was reportedly rescued, while he was swimming in the cold waters of the deep lake. He resumed work after recovering from the minor injuries he sustained.

The whole lake area had always been in control of the Army, a three-day walk away from the nearest road. So more reports about the incident were difficult to obtain, for the journalists, who were mostly crowded in Kathmandu, to report the most trivial matters about the capital. The bodies of the pilot and the royal lady were recovered, though not the remains of the helicopter. She was cremated in the presence of Prince Paras, at Pashupatinath, where he also shed a tear.

She was the youngest sister of the slain Queen Aishwarya, and had practically separated from her husband Prince Dhirendra, who had married a British woman, a few years ago. He lived in London, after he had renounced his royal title and became a commoner. It was during one of the follow-up checks of King Birendra, after his heart-surgery in Britain, that he found his youngest brother living in dire conditions. His British wife had deserted him.

The king asked Dhirendra to return to Nepal, which he did, only to get involved in politics, in a way that the leftist forces were suspected to have joined hands with the royalists, and were about to sink the democratic ones. In spite of his perhaps unhappy marriage, he was a man with shrewd political instincts. So, while Gyanendra and his wife Komal survived, both of their siblings were no more. King Gyanendra declared the new hierarchy of the royal family soon, but refrained from declaring Paras the Crown-prince, for Paras did not have a good public image. He waited till the next Dashain day, which is considered a day to mark the victory of truth over falsehood, by the Hindus.

KING Gyanendra had a business-like air about him. Business was what he was doing, before he became the king. He owned a five-star hotel and several other enterprises, in partnership with a descendant of an earlier Rana. He had also earlier created an image of being a hardliner, by dismissing writers or journalists as mere pen-pushers, in a TV interview. It was a different matter, that he himself wrote poetry. Some of his writings had been published as a book, and a few poems had been adapted into songs. They were not very romantic, and there was a hint of nationalism in most of them.

Once he was seen addressing a group as if monarchy was still absolute in Nepal, many years after monarchy had been replaced by a Constitutional setup. But he was an enigma for most people. He had never been involved in any controversy, on account of his personal conduct. Also, when his grandfather, King Tribhuwan, took refuge with the royal family, in the Indian embassy, before they were all dispatched to India, the ruling Rana elite made Gyanendra ascend the throne as a king, when he has not reached puberty. He was somehow left behind from the crowd of the king's family taking a refuge in India. The king then had almost no power and was like a prisoner inside his palace and in his name the Rana family ruled the country. The throne of the king couldn't be left vacant so Gyanendra was made king by the Ranas.

It was a time of extreme exploitation of the people by the regime. They lived in dire poverty and ignorance in the countryside while the ruling elites in Kathmandu tried to maintain the life of European aristocrats.

King Gyanendra remained the king only for a few months, because soon, Tribhuwan returned and the leading democratic leader B.P. Koirala became the first elected prime minister of Nepal, under a constitutional monarchy after the Rana rulers accepted to continue their rule under a kind of democracy where their feudal powers were reduced and their fate was to be decided by an election. They lost this election by a landslide and Koirala's party won a two-third majority in the parliament.

Thus, more than a century old feudal rule of the Ranas was brought to an end. In their hands, the king had been reduced to a puppet. They forcefully married the royals as per their wish, to consolidate their own position among their family, which had multiplied so much during the decades that the power struggle among them was often settled by massacre of an entire family of a cousin by another.

The British colonials in India appeased the Nepalese Rana rulers by actively participating in the power struggle among the cousins. They favoured the ones who were ruthless enough to exploit their countrymen to fulfil the need of the colonials. It included fighting the World Wars from the British side and suppressing the independence movement of India, led by Mahatma Gandhi in its later phase. Also, Nepalese soldiers were depended on fully, by a few hundred thousand British colonials, to provide them security, to rule India with a population of three hundred million. King Tribhuwan took it no more and sought Indian help to establish a democratic system in Nepal, after the British colonials had left the subcontinent in 1947.

On the day he became king, Gyanendra formed a three member body to investigate the royal massacre. The Chief Justice, the Speaker of the Parliament and the Leader of the Opposition were the members he nominated. They were given the freedom to interrogate the members of the royal family at will, to find out what happened on that Friday evening.

However, the Leader of the Opposition, Madhav, Nepal backed out, saying that the process through which the investigating body had been formed was not valid. Being a communist, he had not shaved his head. His presence in the investigating body might not only have imparted credibility to it, but he could have undertaken a more comprehensive job, if he so desired, to find out what actually transpired. Instead, he denied himself this responsibility, to the disappointment of many people.

The investigating body was reduced to two members, nevertheless it proceeded. It took about a fortnight for it to visit the site of the massacre inside the palace premises, and the army hospital, where the injured royals had been treated. The royals were all interviewed, including the ones who had escaped injuries but were present in the party on that fateful night. Various officials serving in the royal palace and the army hospital were questioned by the investigating body.

Kantipur, a newspaper, published a word-by-word account of all those interviews. The royals interviewed included the only son of Gyanendra, Paras, and Dr Rajiv Shahi, the son-in-law of his younger brother Dhirendra. Both of them were present in the party but survived unhurt. Dr Rajiv already had given a press-conference earlier, at the military hospital where he worked, adding nothing more to what had been so widely reported by the national and international media.

All the interviews conducted by the investigating body, so precisely reported by the newspapers, only supported the earlier theory: an infuriated and intoxicated Crown Prince Dipendra eliminated his entire family. The stated reason was that he was enraged that he not allowed to marry the daughter of Pashupati Samsher Rana, direct descendant of the last ruling Rana family of Nepal before it became a democratic country.

Queen Aishwarya, herself a daughter of the Rana elite, deemed the prince's choice to be of a lesser blood. Family rivalries of the ruling class survived generations.

It was also reported that Dipendra had been continuously in touch with his lover that fateful Friday evening, as the log of his mobile phone calls proved. Panicked by his furious phone calls, she had called Paras and the ADC of Dipendra, warning them that the crown prince was intoxicated and very angry.

On an evening by the end of June that year, when it was pouring very heavily in Kathmandu, the Speaker of the House of Representatives, Tara Nath Ranabhat, presented the report of the investigating body, in the full glare of national and international media. He presented it first in Nepali and then rendered its English translation.

The English translation of the text was so crude that it reported the sound of firing by Dipendra as 'Rat-Rat-Rat', for it was an automatic weapon. It unnecessarily lightened the sombre atmosphere inducing the crowd of reporters present to erupt into fits of laughter. It turned into a comedy, a mere farce, when Ranabhat answered the questions of the reporters, barely able to suppress laughter about to erupt from him, animated by his own humour.

The questions on the findings of the inquest of one of the most tragic incidents in Nepal were answered in a manner which left the officials and the reporters choking with laughter. And to crown it all, this was telecast live. It was a sad commentary on the state of affairs. The report, though, expressed ignorance of the larger motive of Dipendra's action. He was a grown-up man of thirty, not a starry-eyed teenager in love for the first time. Moreover, It was rumoured that he was hardly naïve or innocent, routinely enjoying the services of prostitutes.

Once there appeared an interview of him, in an English newspaper where he said that being a small country, nothing much could be done in Nepal. During that time he was attending the university in Nepal for a post-graduate degree in humanities, which he earned with distinction, later. Living a privileged life possibly had robbed him of the vision necessary to see the power of human efforts. If his interview was indicative of the attitude prevailing in the royal palace, it was not good news, for the people were becoming restless for a change for which the royalty appeared unprepared.

King Birendra had completed his quarter-century as the ruler, for the most part an absolute one, a few years earlier. To mark the occasion, the Nepal Rastra Bank had issued a bank-note of twenty-five rupees and one for two-hundred-fifty rupees. The royals celebrated with a spectacular display of fireworks in the royal palace, one evening. The king, one of the richest men on earth, continued to go to the people in rural areas, who greeted him in their huts, made of stones, wood and mud, themselves in tattered clothes.

It almost looked criminal to be rich among those people. It was often heard however, that Crown Prince Dipendra was an ambitious man, unhappy at the way his father was allowing the political developments to take place. To those close to him, he declared how differently he might have handled the situation, if he was the king. People close to the royal palace, who were losing their privileges, while the democracy was gaining ground, prompted Dipendra to control what they feared was a drift towards democracy.

The development transpired, in the aftermath of the closure of the inquest on the royal massacre, in a way, that Sher Bahadur Deuba became the next prime minister, by ousting Koirala. But Girija Koirala was backing a vote of no confidence against Deuba government. Deuba, now broken away from his party to form a party of his own, recommended the dissolution of Parliament after having drinks with the king one evening. The king accepted his request and the Parliament was dissolved immediately, making Deuba the caretaker PM from an elected one, on the same evening.

The sentimental, plump and balding ambassador of the USA fully backed the Nepalese security forces to eliminate the Maoists. His TV interviews with Bijay Kumar Pandey, a popular television-journalist, appeared often, in which he sounded belligerent against the Maoists. But his tenure was to be over shortly. A tall and lean man replaced him who was not less hostile to the Maoists but was more careful about the things he said in public.

The Royal Nepalese Army had already acquired the American M16 automatic rifles by now, finding that the Indian made ones were inoperable in a combat situation. The new ambassador set conditions for the Maoists to be removed from the USA's terrorists list. In the aftermath of September 11, in the year the king was assassinated in Nepal, after the Twin-Tower had been brought down by terrorist attack in the USA, the US forces were already at war in Afghanistan and Iraq, along with some allied forces. The USA's security policies were tighter than ever.

The caretaker government of Deuba was not able to decide on any matter, to make clear recommendations to the king, on the matter of dealing with the Maoists. The Maoists' extortion and torture of the people in the rural areas seemed to have escalated. The political situation in Kathmandu became unstable by the day. Several people whose legs the Maoists had smashed with a heavy sledge hammer, used in the villages to mould hot iron, were receiving treatment at the teaching hospital at Kathmandu, as per newspaper reports. The Maoists suspected them to be government spies. Using the hammers they pulverised the bones making it near impossible for the doctors to fix them.

In another incident, they killed one of the school-teachers in Gorkha. They took him out of his class, in front of the students, and tied him to a tree. Then they beat him with sticks, to death, because he had declined to part with a quarter of his salary. It was the share the Maoists demanded - and which most of the government employees paid. His dead body tied to a tree appeared on the cover of *Himal* weekly magazine, which was popular at that time. Maoist snipers also killed the chief of armed police force one morning in Kathmandu, along with his wife and bodyguard. They were on a morning walk in the Ring Road area. A few senior army-officers too were similarly killed near their residences.

The violence was reciprocated by the Army. In one instance, a car driver was shot dead by Army troops after his car bumped into an army vehicle plying ahead during the morning rush hour in Kathmandu. In Nagarkot, a soldier opened fire with an automatic weapon on civilians gathered at a temple celebrating a festival, killing nearly a dozen of them indiscriminately. He was earlier among the crowd, where he picked up a fight with a few local youths, who had asked him to keep away from the girls in the crowd, as was reported. He returned to his barracks and brought back the weapon, and then caused the carnage. The Army promised to punish the troops who caused such atrocities.

In one of the pictures appearing in the newspapers during this time were the troops carrying body of a Maoist rebel, killed in an encounter. The hands and feet were tied to a wooden pole and the body was thus carried, just like an animal killed in a hunt.

It was evident that the war was beginning to toughen people on both sides. You were on one side or the other, a Maoist leader declared, there was no middle-ground to tread on for the commoner. People used to fight as mercenaries or for a salary for other countries, but finding a war at their own doorstep they appeared unprepared for the consequences. But possibly it was inevitable. Social conditions make rebels out of emotionally, educationally and financially insecure young men ill-equipped for the life ahead. More so if cultural rituals are the only source of redemption in a life full of turmoil. To kill or get killed for a small salary, inappropriate as it was, was often the only option they had.

Even Nepalese folk-songs betrayed this state of affairs, where dying fighting a war in a far-away setting is romanticised, celebrating the pathos of a dying soldier, fallen by an enemy he does not know at all, sung with heart-rending passion.

While the violence was escalating to victimise the weakest, the British ambassador was as ambivalent as ever. He claimed to have lived in the rural areas of Kathmandu in the north, when he was a young student many decades back. Britain and the USA tried to negotiate the matters of Nepal with India, while the Indian foreign minister Pranab Mukherjee described the problems of Nepal as India's domestic problem.

The right-wing Hindu party led coalition government in India had been voted out of power a while ago. It had fought an election, calling for the elections early, with the slogan of 'shining-India', fully convinced that it would make a clean sweep in the elections. But the Indian voters had a different idea. Earlier, in the previous elections, the escalating cost of onions prior to the elections caused the Congress downfall. A voter with a short memory often acts on whims. But it changes the fortunes of the politicians overnight and drastically.

Congress was now back in power in India, led by a Sikh intellectual as a figurehead PM, while the real power rested with the party president, Sonia Gandhi, the widow of Rajiv Gandhi.

The King of Nepal, Gyanendra, remarkably, had declined to meet the British and the Indian ambassadors, who tried their best, to get an appointment with him, for almost a year now. In one of his rare interviews during this period, the king mentioned how formidable the Nepalese-resistance was. By denying a meeting with the ambassadors of the two countries which were thought to have the biggest influence on Nepal, he was personifying the resistance. He also remarkably mentioned that true virtue lies in having power and not using it.

On a day, as the winter was about to be over, the king sacked the Deuba government and took the executive power in his own hands. Nawin saw a senior official of Royal Nepalese army in his neighbourhood, taking rounds in front of his house, looking at the passerby people vindictively.

Nawin was on his way to submit the application of his younger son at the St. Xavier's school at Jaulakhel, for admission in the first standard. He was aware that this school mostly accepted admissions from people converted to Christianity or who had connections. But he wanted to see if things had changed. His elder son Rahul could not get admission into St. Xavier's five years back.

It was in his earlier days in Kathmandu that Nawin applied for the job of a teacher in St. Xaviers, which he couldn't get. This school was preferred by people for their children's education as it had properly trained teachers and enough space for all kinds of activities which took place in a school. Its Higher Secondary classes ran from its Maiti Ghar campus, which had proper science labs. But its entrance examinations became more and more controversial over the years.

A significant number of new schools owned by the private sectors had cropped up in the city. They worked hard and were getting good results too. But they had very little space and as a result appeared too crowded. Besides they were situated in the commercial areas of the city in congested or far off places. So, St. Xavier's was the first preference of most parents for the education of their children.

Just as he was leaving home, his landlord uncharacteristically called him from behind, to ask if he had not heard that the king had taken over the state power, as announced by Radio Nepal. He suggested it would be better to stay indoors on such a day. Nawin said that he was aware of that but he had to submit the application at the school as it was the last day.

It was a warm day after a cold morning. Nawin decided to go to the school walking, as he had planned, instead of returning and remaining at home, fearing the anarchy and violence in the streets on account of the king's action.

On the way he saw the crowded school buses rushing back from the schools, to drop the children home. Panic was there in the air, most people were rushing home. But the school Nawin went to was open and accepted the application he had come to submit. He returned walking back in the sun. As it appeared to him later, it was useless to fear the unknown, when the day passed without any major incident.

An emergency had been declared by the new regime. Civilian communication, which included mobile telephones and the Internet now, was denied for about a week. During this period the security forces searched the offices of different news media owned by the private sector. Censorship prompted *The Kathmandu Post*, an English daily, to write an editorial on socks, among other things; while the popular community FM radio channel Sagarmatha broadcast an article on cow. The signs were clear that the people would not take it easily anymore if the new king tried to dismantle democracy, as his father Mahendra did, nearly half-a-century ago.

The old faces, prime ministers during the period the king directly ruled through a party-less Panchayati system, became the new PMs, one after another. Tulsi Giri, once a Home Minister of Nepal, who was responsible for the undoing of the democracy during the rule of King Mahendra, was brought back by the king, from Bengaluru in India, where he was living in self-imposed exile. He was always mentioned in the political discussions in Nepal, though he was not seen publicly for almost fifty years. So there was some mystery about him in the minds of the recent generation. He was expected to manage and manipulate the similar trick once again, that of causing long-term damage to the democracy.

However, it was discovered that he had some loans outstanding from the government-owned banks, since the time he was here earlier. In the days and months which followed, this became a major point for the newspapers to criticise Tulsi Giri. The pressure of the media made him pay back the loans, with interest. So, instead of making some money out of the political predicament of Nepal, for a change, he was made to pay his due.

The time seemed to have changed a lot than he assumed. An old, decrepit man with false teeth and multiple marriages, Giri sounded rhetorical when he told the media that he did not have enough power like before, to deal with the present situation. He looked disappointed to have discovered that King Gyanendra was not like his father, King Mahendra. For one, the new king was not a natural successor in the royal palace, and for another it was a new century. His speech distorted during the interview due to his efforts to keep his ill-fitting artificial dentures in place. Tulsi Giri deteriorated into a figure of comedy from one of awe. However, people like Binod Shah, who were close to the palace earlier, when the king ruled directly, became politically active yet again.

Ministers too changed very often. In a way they represented the people of the society the king knew personally and considered them worthy of assisting him loyally, in ruling the country. But, to a commoner, they were either a part of the plutocracy the monarchy had built over the last few decades it was ruling the country without interruption, ever since after King Tribhuwan returned from India; after he took a refuge in the Indian embassy at Kathmandu and subsequently in India; and negotiated his return home with the help of Indian government. Some of the ministers during this time were simply royal relatives.

A few weeks later, Nawin took his younger son on his motorbike to St. Xavier's school to appear in the Entrance Examination for Class I.

When he reached its front office he was told that it was to take place in a hall located on the back, next to the football ground. He took out his parked motorbike and took his son to the narrow road next to the Zoo, from where the football ground of the school was near.

There they saw that the road was overcrowded with parked vehicles. It was difficult to miss that people had money in Kathmandu now, as there were so many shining cars and SUVs of the renowned companies, parked there. In spite of all the trouble the country faced, the economy was growing rapidly.

The consumption of oil and power was doubling every two years. It was the most potent sign of growth.

He found a place to stand his motorbike with a little effort. They found the football ground overcrowded, when they reached it, with parents and their children. They were mostly eating dry foods from the packets and drinking cold drinks. It looked more like a festival to Nawin, than an examination day, where people were more interested to see and to be seen. Besides it was Saturday: a weekly holiday.

The exam was taking place in several schedules throughout the day. There were thousands of applicants for a few hundred seats.

Nawin found the seat of his son and left him to sit for the exam lasting an hour. His son liked the place and was in a happy mood. Nawin waited for him in the football field like other parents, wondering how good it looked between the surroundings so crowded. Empty spaces were rare in Kathmandu with the property prices skyrocketing with each passing day.

Soon his son returned and told Nawin that he had fared well. They returned home where Rahul and Aarti were waiting for them.

The results came after a few days. There was no surprise for Nawin. His younger son too couldn't make it to St. Xavier's school.

Every winter people in the country faced load shedding half the time, as the rivers dried up after the monsoons and power generation plummeted. One of the energy-ministers, the one in office in the king's government, who also traded in generators, among other machines and automobiles, and was a notable businessman of the country, advised the people to buy generators, when he was asked how people should cope with the deficient power supply. Not minding the fact that the supply of petroleum products was sporadic at best, in the country, as the Girija-led government had earlier given monopoly to India to supply the same, through a very controversial treaty.

But it was not to become a big issue, as even less than twenty per cent people had electric power supplied to their homes. Though there were some visionary people in the villages, who already were harvesting solar power, high up in the hills; which was not yet fashionable even in the capital of the country, where people waited for the government to solve their problems. They were though, either foreign-educated people, choosing to live in their native villages, or were retired soldiers of British-Gorkha army - generally those who had a glimpse of the larger world of the twenty first century.

Another minister, appointed by the king, a renowned physician, had reportedly got a tarred road built in his village in a remote district. But only until it reached his house, his next-door neighbour reportedly complained.

The attitude responsible for bringing the society to such a pass seemed to persist even among the people educated in some of the most renowned universities abroad. Contrary to what the king might have thought, when he overtook the executive power of the state, he appeared to be having a limited choice.

As time passed the ministers changed more frequently, indicating that the king was getting desperate, for the insurgency made it difficult for the rusted machinery of the government to function.

The king however, gave the decisive power to the army to deal with the Maoists. The war escalated, as the army went on an offensive. It was no more waiting for the guerrillas to attack. Instead it was going deeper into the forests to destroy their bases. The army was finally becoming a fighting force from a ceremonial one which people joined earlier to periodically join the UN peace-keeping missions, to earn them a middle class life. There were search operations during the nights in Kathmandu, during which many people disappeared. The ranks of Army swelled apart from the budget it needed. Additional ration of one hundred grams of dry-fruits per day was provisioned for the soldiers, as it was decided that the routine ration was deficient in calories to fight a war. But half the people of the country continued to live under chronic food-scarcity and occasional famine.

The king's takeover of power prompted a number of political leaders to flee to India. Among them was the daughter of Girija Koirala. And also a writer/journalist fled to India, who was the daughter of a staunch royalist, who was a minister in the royal-government. She got herself injured and photographed in *Kantipur* earlier, while taking part in a demonstration against the rule of the king. If the option of flight was excluded somehow, the narratives of politics and literature of the country might have been different.

But modern times keep one constantly flirting with the thought of flight, more so if one is made to feel as if one does not belong to the place one was born or lives in. It was so when colonialism and slavery are said to have ended. A popular vernacular columnist vandalised the venue, along with a crowd he was leading, to disrupt the 'Miss Nepal' contest being held there. He had argued earlier that such contests were against Nepalese culture. Words seemed to have lost their meanings and only actions, visible and violent, seemed to matter. His was an honest response to the crisis everyone was feeling in the country, not defiled with a possibility of the flight. The sting from his writing was to be taken away later, however, when his children flew away to foreign lands, to seek a career.

It became almost impossible to restrict the freedom of Press. The unrestrained ventilation of popular sentiments through the media made sure that the king remained less than a dictator. But newspapers were full of propaganda also. Some of it by foreign commentators deeply entrenched in their European-city, who apparently had no idea about either Nepal or the Nepalese. They wanted to see victory of the left in the Nepalese Maoist war, after it was apparently faltering in South America.

Young people from Kathmandu, who probably had not missed a breakfast on account of the Maoist-war, as the capital city was the least affected by it - and the people from the hinterland were pouring into it, due to the security it provided - were migrating to the cities in Europe or the USA or Canada, as refugees. Ironically, as if making room for the real refugees in Kathmandu.

Some of them were publishing columns in the newspapers in Kathmandu, often in English, trying to make the war continue, through their specious arguments, as it guaranteed their new life as refugees in Europe or the USA. They were the first to speak against any peace-initiative, the ones which were often aired by the concerned people in Nepal. Similarly, the Nepalese settled abroad in comfortable jobs, but still interested in the politics at home, too wrote columns with similar intentions. Such writing however, often betrayed how little these people knew about their own country. The idea of witnessing a war, though among their own people, from a safe place had corrupted them.

THE road to Kathmandu from Narayangarh was blocked for three days due to a landslide caused by heavy rains. It was September and the monsoon could stretch into October. 'Come September, the economy will improve,' once a harassed finance minister of India said, irked by the strident criticism of him for not being able to arrest inflation.

In Nepal too, inflation was twice the rate-of-growth, for the past few years. Given the fact that growth benefited only the chosen few, while inflation hurt everyone, it was clear that a few people were being patronised by the government at the cost of the rest. Newspapers were busy painting a brighter picture of the future, on account of the growth. They downplayed or ignored the inflation in their editorials, while advertising or publishing reviews only of the books on spirituality, published in English often by a German publisher.

The chief of Indian Planning Commission had reduced the criteria of poverty from a dollar a day income to nearly half. In statistics it reduced the poverty by nearly twenty-five per cent. There were, however, seventy billionaires for seven hundred million Indians living below poverty line, as it was heading towards seven decades of its independence.

As an aftermath, students of a leading technical institute in India declined to receive their degrees from the prime minister, who was the chief guest of the convocation ceremony there. The democracy was becoming a ritual of voting, though a few commentators wrote in newspapers, that nearly a trillion dollars have been stashed away in the banks of a country like Switzerland, by the Indian ruling class, during the two decades after the economic reforms began.

Like a woman in the hands of an impotent man, it was not bearing any fruit - a commentator said, in a debate on a FM radio channel, about the state of democracy in Nepal. Being so much influenced by India, Nepal had almost a similar political system in place. It entailed that many anomalies prevalent in India were beginning to appear in the Nepalese system too. The constitutional mechanisms to man them were not allowed to work by the ruling elites, as it could have undone them. A periodic election gave a legality to this scheme.

Indeed, September represented monsoons and fertility. A good rain could mean a better agricultural output and a hope of reduction in food prices and the money going back to the farmers in the rural sector, albeit in small amounts. From there it was again sucked back into the cities, by the ruthless policies of the government. But its mere circulation back in the rural areas helped the economy, which was best secured by a good rainfall, rather than the policies of the government.

Unexceptionally, the cities were over-crowded. They were the centres of educational opportunities, medical treatment, and investment or employment; or of politics and economy - in general. Occasionally, a prudent columnist in a newspaper also described a city as a monstrous head in the emaciated body of a malnourished child in a famine hit area.

Nawin was returning to Kathmandu. Since the road was blocked, the choice was either to wait for it to get cleared or take a detour of around two hundred kilometres south, and try to reach Kathmandu through the old highway, from Hetauda. The possibility was there that the rains could block that highway too. Trendy, brand new Japanese mini-buses were collecting passengers willing to take the detour.

'Only five hundred rupees sir! By the time it is dark you will be in Kathmandu. You can see it's a brand new vehicle for a comfortable journey. You will feel like a tourist!' the helper boy of the minibus persuaded Nawin. Recent changes in the system had brought prosperity among the people and many of them became entrepreneurs, running services like this minibus, ready to cater to the impromptu. Nawin tried to bargain the cost a little. But the helper was adamant.

He decided to move, instead of anxiously watching and waiting in a hotel. Action often appeared more compulsive than thought, for it visibly engaged one and all. On the outskirts of Narayangarh were traffic policemen, who extracted a fixed bribe from the minibuses, for running on a route for which they had no permit. A three days' road-block had already put in place an alternative of the usual, which benefited the ones in the government, and the entrepreneurs, who could sense the opportunity. After that they just sailed.

The climb began from Hetauda and it continued till they reached two thousand five hundred meters at Palung. The mountains suddenly became enveloped in clouds and it started to rain. The wind became chilly.

Earlier, Nawin had a fever when he got down at Gorakhpur, off a train from Mumbai. He had changed his job again some time ago and had joined an Indian company.

It was a low fever with body-aches, which left him worried if he had caught one of the diseases carried by mosquitoes or through dirty drinking-water in India.

He reached Bhairahawa with difficulty and was unable to proceed further. He decided to rest in a hotel till he felt better. After two days and taking the medicines the hotel-attendant bought for him, from a medicine shop, he felt better. It had been raining incessantly throughout, during this period. He occasionally came out of his room to have a look at the surroundings, from the balcony of the hotel. But the visibility was limited due to rain. He finally had a little food after almost forty-eight hours. Returning appetite was a sign of health. The next morning he had a bowel movement, the first in three days. It was yet another sign of recovery. He decided to take the next available bus to Kathmandu.

By afternoon he reached Narayangarh. All the places he went through were hot and humid in September, whether in India or Nepal. This detour was unexpected, and he had no warm clothes. He shivered as a cold wind blew into the bus. When it stopped to take a break, the passengers went for toilets and snacks. Nawin decided on heavy snacks and a few cups of black tea. He still felt weak. The cost of food available had multiplied, as this kind of traffic on the detour was unexpected. The people selling food at eating places wanted to make the most of it.

When the journey resumed he felt better. It was due to the hot food and the hope that by evening he would be with his family.

A fortnight of hectic journey and the official meetings in Mumbai, where the Head Office of the pharmaceutical company he worked for now was located, had resulted in a fever, which had confined him for two additional days at a hotel.

He took a tour in Mumbai whenever he was free, to see this fabled city. It was incredibly crowded and filthy: unlike anything he had heard about it. He once boarded a steamer to have a ride of a few hours in the sea from The Gateway of India. The gate was built to welcome King George V of England, when he came to India.

After several kilometres into the sea, Nawin was surprised that there was a change in the colour of water. It became clear blue from murky green. He was told by someone that all the filth of the city of fifteen million people is directly dumped into the sea. So it was dirty near the coast.

Also, he read the newspaper reports that about a dozen people die in road and train accidents everyday in Mumbai. On visiting the museum of the city, Nawin discovered that nearly a quarter of the articles on display were from Nepal. They were Buddhist paintings or embroidery mostly. The museums in Kathmandu, Lalitpur and Bhaktpur were full of them. As usual, it was depressing to be in a big city in this part of the world, which preyed on the energies of the people it attracts from the impoverished rural areas surrounding it, through its seductive charm promising affluence and fame. A promise often proved false for most of the migrants. Nawin wanted to be back home with his family.

He struck up a conversation with the young man who was sharing the seat with him. To his pleasant surprise, he was from Darchula, a place next to Baitadi, his home district. They began talking in their native language. He told Nawin that he was barely twenty-one years old and was about to complete his sixth year of service in the Army.

'I had no choice. The Maoists came to our village, pressuring young boys like me to join them. Our parents hid us or we ran away to the forests near our village, when they came. Some of my unfortunate friends were caught by them and taken away. Most of them died within a week. With no training they were asked to ambush the military or armed police posts.

'They were also used as human-shields, to make the security forces run out of rounds, before the guerrillas started the real attack. Some of my friends ran away to the Indian cities like

Delhi or Bombay, if they had a relation there. I was about to appear in the School Leaving Certificate exam the next summer. But I had no choice except to give up my studies. One night I ran away to the district headquarters, when someone told me that the army recruitment was taking place.

'During that time it was difficult to find recruits for the Army, because as you know ....,' and he pulled and released his bent right index finger, as if on a trigger. 'There were reports of Army men deserting. But I joined it. After a training of just six months I was deployed on active duty.

'Once the Maoist ambushed one of our outposts at night, where I was also deployed. Three of my friends were killed before we started to fire back. The Maoists ran out of rounds soon and we went after them. We killed a dozen of them, though most of them ran away. These days, when things have calmed down a little, there is a crowd of boys willing to join the Army. They often pay bribes too. But during those days there was almost no competition.

'I used to search the passenger buses during the day, passing through the highway near our post. I saw many of the faces from my village; which, as I had heard, had joined the Maoists. I could have apprehended them and they might have certainly been killed. But I let them go, seeing the entreaty in their eyes and their bodies shivering with fear. After all, we were from the same village. I thought why kill each other for a war that has no purpose,' he said ironically.

The sky had cleared by then. The sun illuminated the white Himalayas and the green hills before them, far away in the east. The bus was passing though the beautiful Daman valley, which was in the shadow of a western mountain rising high above it. The fields next to the town were full of green vegetables. Next to them was a dense forest. Nawin thought about the loss of adolescence of the man, a war veteran at a very young age. The minibus descended, as it became dark, into Teestung, famous for supplying vegetables to Kathmandu.

On reaching Naubise, just twenty kilometres short of Kathmandu, where both the highways met, Nawin and other passengers discovered that the other highway too had opened. So their taking the detour of two hundred kilometres was unnecessary. Some of the passengers cursed the helper of the minibus, who misinformed them about the extent of the landslide and speculated that the roadblock may continue for another three days, before he hustled them back to the bus.

'LONG time, no see?' said Dilip, on meeting Nawin near a bank's office at New Road.

'That is the *khusi*,' replied Nawin, winking. *Khusi* meant happiness, in Nepali.

Dilip's face distorted, due to his efforts to suppress the laughter on hearing it. They shook hands, the feeling of companionship as alive as ever, though they were meeting after a long time. Nawin noted that Dilip had gained more weight than was suitable for his age and wore the round Gandhi-glasses, in a frame of plastic and not steel. His back-combed thick hair mostly had lost its artificial colouring and was grey near the roots, over his high forehead. His double chin betrayed that he had had a comfortable life. The smile of his clean-shaven face further gave him away by making him look like a banker, who was speculated to be the highest-paid employee in the country; collecting his enormous cheeks over it, pushing the Gandhi-glasses upwards.

'Let us go and see the Kaisher Library, we talked about last time. I am sure being a lazy person, you have not been there, in spite of my persuasion,' Dilip suggested, as high spirited as ever.

Nawin nodded and followed him, as the library was a few minutes' walk away. On the way Dilip explained how he successfully persuaded one of the women, who was a receptionist at the office of the newspaper he was working with, at present, to take naked pictures of herself on his mobile phone. He handed his cell phone to Nawin, who reluctantly looked at a few of the photos before returning the mobile to Dilip.

'I want to make a sex video with her,' Dilip said.

'Really? For what?'

'To upload on the Internet and share with my friends. You know she is interested in the reality-shows on TV and wants to become a star.'

'But your video will make her a star of different kind. Will she agree to that?'

'Let us see. I am persuading her. I hope she will agree. After all, it is a global trend.'

'You heard the news that a Chinese man watched the porn movie for the first time and found his wife with his best friend in it? You too plan to give a similar surprise to someone?' Nawin asked, a little dismayed.

'No. She is still not married, and does not want to marry ever. As she says, becoming a star is her dream,' Dilip replied after laughing. They walked in silence for a while.

'But what about you? You want to be a writer, exposing yourself in a sex tape...'

'It is an age of e-books Nawin. Books are no longer physical objects only. Don't you see how books promoted by a celebrity on a talk show become bestsellers? People like authors to perform on stage, before they buy their books. Once you see an author performing on stage you understand what the writing might be. Therefore people buy expensive e-book readers to download the free books. Authors are almost a dispensable species now.

'Reading is a rigorous exercise. More so when junk food is the main health hazard people face. So, releasing your sex tape before your book may prove a solid PR exercise for an author. I want to be the pioneer of this trend,' Dilip said. Nawin felt as if his heart had missed several beats. He spoke no more.

They passed a small temple next to the busy road. A girl in low-cut pants was offering prayers sitting on her knees. Every time she bowed to touch the ground in front of the idols of the deities with her forehead, the split of the bottom was revealed. Passers-by looked at her with interest. Her efforts to cover her lower back drew more attention.

'How busy are you?' Nawin asked.

'Not much. I have to do a feature on the Kaisher library for this weekend's issue of my paper. I will just go there to see what I can write about it,' Dilip replied. 'This is how a journalist works: Looks around for stories all the time.'

They walked on, feeling nice in the warming sun of the winter day. There were more people on the roads now. Sweepers had already cleared the human excreta which had collected during the night on the pavements in front of Bir hospital and the Durbar High School. The cleaners had spread lime-powder to clean the spots from where they had cleared the filth.

Lepers were begging on a side of the hospital, among them was a person with a monstrous elephant-leg, displaying it to beg.

There were people selling Chinese or Indian goods on the footpath. A Chinese man had attracted a crowd. Sitting on a stool, he cut open a shoe with a knife and then pasted together the opened part with a solution he squeezed out of a tube. 'Tansi ... Tansi ...' he shouted to the crowd. Probably it was the only Nepali word he knew. It meant stick together. People were impressed. A few of them purchased the tube of the solution he was selling, every time he demonstrated its effect.

Next to him were the Indian or Nepalese fortune-tellers in their saffron dresses. They sat on cushions on the ground. Most of them had a bird in a cage beside them. The bird came out, walking, when a fortune-teller opened its cage's small door.

The bird would pick an envelope from a bundle of many. The bird walked back to the cage to be locked in once again, after the fortune-teller collected from its beak the envelope and it also had picked up a few grains of rice it was rewarded with, by the fortune-teller; from one of the small boxes in front of him, displayed on a mattress on the ground. Most of those boxes contained chewing-tobacco earlier.

The fortune-teller locked the cage. Then he carefully took out a card from the envelope, to read from it the fortune of his customer, who was anxiously waiting, sitting in front of the fortune-teller on another cushion. The fortune-tellers also had several colourful stones in the rings of metal and the garlands of rudraksha seeds. These were charms, to sell to their customers, who became convinced after listening to their fortune that they needed a protection from evil spirits.

Some people sold bottles filled with colourful liquids and dried herbs of different hues, as a treatment for various ailments ranging from gastric problems to premature ejaculation. On their small loudspeakers they made extraordinary claims about the potency of their medicines, particularly the ones for sexual problems. They used voices mimicking popular politicians.

'Have you ever tried Viagra?' Dilip asked suddenly, with a smile which ironically was shy and caused dimples on his reddened cheeks.

'No. I have never tried it. What about you?' Nawin asked.

'I did. Yes. But a long time ago, when it was newly introduced in the market and a friend of mine brought me a few pills from the USA. Even Bob Dole, the Republican Presidential candidate against Bill Clinton, claimed to have used it then. He was in his sixties and was a war-veteran. It gave me an erection which shocked my lover of those days. She was a newlywed and lived in a village with her in-laws on the way to Gokarna.

'On the first day I tried Viagra with her, she thought I was a different man. She asked me to take a shower to subside the erection.'

'Really? I think you are exaggerating.'

'You may not believe, but it is true. Mind you, it was the original American Viagra pills I am talking about. Nowadays you have so many imitations on the market, made in either China or India. They are not even half as effective and cost less than a cigarette!'

'Or, maybe you are older than before,' Nawin added with malice.

'These matters are very risky you know!' Dilip smiled. 'There was a crime in a village in the outskirts of Kathmandu some time back. A man and his wife and two young children were stabbed to death one night. To this day the police have no clue about the crime. However, it was discovered that the man murdered had sexual relationship with most of the young women in the village.'

The library was at the next crossing of Jamal. It was indeed in a big building. The entrance to the library itself was from a room which might have been the drawing-room of Kaisher Rana. There were tiger skins or deerskin on the floor, on the carpet. Small, black and white, framed pictures of the Rana elite adorned one of the walls.

Some pictures showed a crowd of wives of a Rana around him, apart from their children; in others, a Rana had his foot on the body of a tiger or a wild-buffalo, hunted-down, with the rifle in his hand. Stuffed whole-animal skins of different species adorned the drawing-room, with their jaws and claws intact. Stuffed-heads of wild-cats and buffaloes occupied a wall on one side, their glass-eyes staring blankly at visitors.

There were also life-sized oil paintings, portraits of the ancestors of Kaiser Rana, wearing their military regalia and colourful turbans, a sword supporting them while they stood. The sofas and carpets were damaged though, as were the beautifully carved wooden-chairs, which Nawin thought needed immediate maintenance.

In the gallery next to the drawing-room were the library shelves, containing many books. Many of them leather-bound and printed in the USA or UK, at the turn of the last century, or later; as Dilip had said. Towards the end of the gallery were photographs of great leaders of the world, above the book-shelves. They included a picture of the Indian leader Nehru in front of a board which proclaimed 'Photography Strictly Prohibited,' in English and Hindi. Nawin looked at Dilip, expecting some comment. But he was so reverentially observing the picture that he perhaps did not notice the notice. Next to it were pictures of British and Japanese monarchs, apart from the Chinese leaders like Chou En Lai and Mao Tse Tung.

'To this day, leather remains a symbol of luxury,' Nawin said, while they browsed the books in the gallery. 'Have you noticed the stuffed animals in the drawing-room?'

'You know, in England in a library is a book, bound in human-leather, of a slave. It feels grainy on touching, *The Times of India* reported. An English philosopher once said that many books do not represent an enlightened age.'

They remained silent while they looked at some of the books. They lingered longest in front of the fiction section of the library and promptly left the section which had the books on science.

'Publishing a book is no big deal. You need to have a clever marketing plan to sell it. I have thought about donating a quarter of the royalty from my books to a charity like the one helping the trafficked-women in Nepal. You know Prince Charles also sells the painting he makes in England to help this charity here. Middle-class people have a fetish for charity no less strong than the royals. They also buy books to indulge. My book, when published, will prove a big success,' Dilip said, breaking the silence.

Nawin felt irritated on hearing it. Dilip seemed to have every plan about his book except writing it. He noticed that Dilip was not wearing the charm he saw last time. 'What happened to the charm you used to wear in your neck?' he asked.

'Oh, don't ask about that. The Guru turned out to be a fraud. It was discovered that he used to hire prostitutes to have sex in the towns where he conducted his meditation sessions. Now the doctor I was seeing too has stopped following him. But both the Guru and the doctor are rich,' Dilip said ironically.

With some difficulty they were able to find a restaurant, amongst the massage-parlours-cum-restaurants and the shops selling curio items or the equipment for mountaineering or other adventure sports. Dilip dropped hints that he was expecting to go to the USA to take a short course in journalism at a university.

'I would have liked to get an extended visa to undertake a graduate course there. But that is not possible. The US embassy is very selective in giving the visa here. What you think it will be like to attend a university in the USA for six months? Did not you try to go there on a student visa and then get a permanent one to settle there? You must have noticed most of the people try to do that. It is so obvious for people like us,' he said.

'I do not know what I will study at a university there. If you are not going to study a subject in science, going to a US university is of no use,' Nawin replied. 'At our age masturbation too may prove equally educative,' he added, almost shocking Dilip out of his breath. Dilip remained silent after that for some time.

The restaurant owner was reluctant to serve only tea. He was expecting customers who would ask for beer instead, for it was already evening, so that he could make some real money. Selling tea alone was not profitable enough for him to run the restaurant. 'Maza lena hai pine ka to kam dhire dhire pi...' the ghazal of Indian singer Pankaj Udhas was playing on a low volume. It meant: if you want to enjoy drinks take small sips, slowly.

'You know why the whites or tourists are called *Kuere* here? It is because they frequent the curio shops,' said Nawin, trying to humour a shocked Dilip and smiling at his own joke.

Dilip laughed nervously, holding a tea-cup in his hand. 'I am intrigued by the Nepalese who go around with a water-bottle in their hands. It was not fashionable earlier. Do you think people here have picked it from the tourists?'

'May be they have. But bottled-water had been more often found with E.Coli, than tap-water, the bacteria responsible for causing diarrhoea. If you go to the outskirts of Kathmandu you will find people filling the twenty-litre containers with water from a stream and then bringing truck-loads of it, sealing it with a blue tape and selling it as mineral water.'

'Since there is no tap-water in Kathmandu in some areas, it does not surprise me. But you know the Americans drank bottled-water supplied by France in a huge quantity until very recently. They thought it had some curative properties, for it was extracted from a particular source in France. The French are so clever at selling things they pack in a bottle. Only when it was found to be contaminated with some toxic minerals that those people started drinking their own American-water, though in bottles once again. I try to avoid bottled-water, as it seems to me an ugly pretentiousness, caused by a newfound prosperity.'

Nawin nodded. 'Yes, that is correct. I have several friends who do not drink tap-water which is available to them. They like the boys delivering them the bottled-water from their bicycles, in the cold Kathmandu mornings. They then put them upside-down on a dispenser.

'I think washing hands often and using toilet paper instead of water to wash every time you defecate will save more lives in

Nepal. It is also important where you defecate. For people living on higher hills might be defecating near the stream from where the people harvest water to bottle in the lower lands. But in the hills the situation is different. People use the latrines made for them by some NGOs from the EU nations to keep their livestock. They are habituated to defecate near their houses, as it proves that they have enough to eat in a famine prone area. It is another matter that in other areas of the country people are declaring their villages as "free-of-faeces-in-the-open". The people so worried about either having enough food or managing their filth are difficult to manage for any type of government.'

'I think civilisation is about how you defecate and avoid having unwanted-children,' Nawin could sense his sarcasm when he said it. He was agitated by the things he was saying.

'What do you mean?' Dilip asked coolly, not caring about his anger.

'All the great communist leaders are products of the families or societies over-run by unwanted children. Their enemies are those who are able to control their fertility and enjoy sex at the same time.' Nawin hoped that it would shut Dilip up and he will not further probe him on this topic.

'You mean it is not about money? Noam Chomsky recently said....' Dilip persisted.

'No. It is about anarchy and order. Money comes later, when you have some order in your life. Do not you see? All the communist victories have led to a greater misery of the ordinary people, and created dictators who were merciless in eliminating whoever even slightly challenged their hold on power? - About Chomsky, I am struck by how identical they look - I mean the leftist intellectuals worldwide - with their plastic rimmed glasses and square jaws. They are well-fed and usually have a comfortable life, talking similar things that do not mean much.

'Prof. Chomsky is a harmless, co-opted critic of the system, as he comes to know a trend ten years after it has passed. For example nowadays he is saying that media is being manipulated by the vested interests, when Rupert Murdoch has himself become Page 3 news, disgraced by being questioned in the glare of the media. Maybe ten years later Chomsky will discover that people have stopped believing what the news says. His books are for the people like Hugo Chavez to wave in the UN conference, when they fall short of words to prove a thing against the USA. Have you read one?'

'No. But seriously Nawin, the things you said while we were in the library were unusual. Do you really think that the European art and culture are on a decline now, apart from their economy?' Dilip asked, trying to suppress his laughter. The seriousness of Nawin, he found, betrayed him the most. He thought Nawin did not mean a single word he said. But talking with him was very amusing for Dilip, who himself read and produced a lot of words everyday, being a journalist. He just had become indifferent to most of them.

Nawin sensed the ridicule in Dilip's manners, which changed often when they were together, as betrayed by the change in his voice. He recalled how tired he himself felt listening to BBC World service on radio only after a few programmes, which mostly reported a crisis in Africa or China, or speculated for about an hour about the changing weather pattern of England in April. He had given up watching it on TV because the visuals were a double-distraction. Poor man, he has to follow and report the news in his job, Nawin thought sympathetically. Dilip too partially shared his scepticism of the things said using English language, he thought, smiling cynically to himself.

'However, being a journalist,' Nawin said, 'can you not see that your Nepalese currency has lost ten per cent of its value against the dollar during the time you were writing the columns in your paper, worrying over the financial problems of Europe and the USA. Why you journalists are so worried about their problems that you cannot see your own?'

'What about the literature they create?' Dilip asked, his eyes narrowing behind his Gandhi-glasses in anger.

'You mean the crime-thrillers and the occult-ones? Very well. People have to refer to books published half-a-century or more ago, to find a genuine literature. Or they have to read the translated Russian literature created even before that. I have not come across a good literature more recently.'

'It is because of the moguls like Rupert Murdoch that the things have declined so much. Everything published was controlled to avoid unnecessary problems. The last five decades were worst, if you think in terms of art or literature. The total defeat of the great powers like Germany and Japan in war has made the world devoid of an alternate in art too.

'People have turned so much inwards that they have lost track of the wider world. It reflects in their recent literature, even in German or Spanish. They dislike English literature certainly, but are not able to provide something better. Popular culture represented by show-business in English seems to have seeped into their world too, as a country like England is also considered as a soft-power nowadays. So now the Germans and Japanese too create a literature they hope will one day be translated into English and sold.'

'But you cannot deny that Germans are enterprising. Recently a German company introduced into the market toilet-papers with poetry of people like Goethe printed on them. It wanted the German people to appreciate their great poets and make some money. But it never took off. People perhaps hold their poets in higher esteem than that company thought. But the Russians are wiser, who have the lines of their great poets printed in their metro railways,' Dilip said.

Nawin ignored it and continued. 'You cannot expect original literature in English from the former colonies of Britain. Most of it is created to impress the English by the spectacular use of the language, often to describe a city like London. But you cannot blame the writers. After all, they need to have their publishing contracts and the awards, which are generally for the English writers of British Commonwealth nations only.

'I meet a Briton sometime, who is not happy to know that I could speak German too. He is annoyed when he is replied in English by the Nepalese, when he tries to practise his Nepali with them,' Nawin continued. 'I am yet to meet one who doesn't think that every Nepalese is a Gurkha who will sacrifice his life for the British Monarch without a second thought. Meanwhile the ex or present Gurkha soldiers are battling with the British government in the courts in London, for equal salary and benefits. Their fabled bravery has plummeted to the extent that a Gurkha soldier was reported to have decapitated a dead Taliban in Afghanistan recently, after a battle.

'I have found this attitude about Nepalese being the Gurkhas in some of the Indians, too. The educated type of them often behave as if they were British or Americans. It could be on account of their ability to speak English. But they can't fool their neighbours.

'If you send away the colonials you do it like Robert Mugabe of Zimbabwe, and begin from scratch. If you rule through the institutions built by the colonials you find that a new breed of native colonials emerges. They are so blatant in exploiting their brethren that people may think their real colonial masters were benign in comparison. But Britain was surprised in Libya. When it realised the need to improve relations with this oil-rich nation, by releasing the Locker-bee bombing convict and asking the son of Colonel Gaddaffi to speak at the London School of Economics, a revolution undid the regime and the Gaddafi family.

'Maybe it is there, I mean the original literature, in vernaculars in these countries, that no one reads. Everything seems to have become an extension of the show-business due to these trends. People do not want to tax their mind. Don't you see how many self-help books are the best-sellers? People want to be guided or patronised through a book. They seek wisdom in it, thinking writers are wise people. They are therefore, happy with what they have been served, regimented thoughts by cultivated writers,' Nawin said, getting irritated at his compulsive speech and the questions of Dilip, 'and the plunder of the world during this time was greater than during colonialism. It all benefited only a few Moguls. That is why I said there could be a revolution in Europe, with Germany financing it.'

'But Rupert Murdoch has fallen and the Russian literature is over-rated. It is more popular in translation elsewhere than in Russian in Russia,' Dilip challenged him further.

'That is why I am not totally pessimistic. I am waiting for others to fall: People, institutions or countries. It all is based on an enormous falsity and cruelty. It cannot last. I hope to find a better literature in the coming days, when "How-to" or "recipe-books" are no more considered a substitute,' Nawin said.

'You make things look so complex,' Dilip said dismissively. He was unwilling to talk on this topic further. Nawin felt provoked to talk more.

'An issue of the newspaper you work for costs less than a cup of tea you are drinking but even as scrap it will be more valuable. That explains the poverty of the people like you and all those in the business of newspapers, except their owners and the advertisers. Who do you think is behind all this? They are people with vested interests in continuing the things as they are. You can push the pen - or play with the key-board - for the rest of your life but the things will not change. If you became experimental, you risk starvation. An educated person like you will certainly prefer poverty.'

Dilip wanted to leave by now. He was breathing heavily to control his anger. Just as a passing thought he asked, 'What you think about "Wikileaks", by the way?'

Nawin did not blink. 'Oh, it is an extension of present day journalism, but more fraudulent. Did you notice it has nothing about a tragedy like Royal Massacre in Nepal? Its leaks are what the people knew throughout. Also, since it involved sex and money, it has itself become news on Page 3. That is the only readable page you have in the newspapers, where who-stripped-today is the news.'

Dilip stood.

He said that he had to attend a dinner at a five star-hotel, where a new car was being launched by a Japanese company. His story on it would appear in tomorrow's newspaper. He shook hands with Nawin, more in control of his emotions now, and left after paying the bill.

He left Nawin behind, who shook his head in disbelief and anger.

For Dilip his profession was fine for himself, as he was able to give time to a friend like Nawin when it was needed. Writing stories about the banal everyday politics was not so inspiring, but very often there was a corruption scandal or a high profile murder or a deadly accident, any of which gave him a chance to use his language enterprisingly. Once, as a bonus, an actress killed herself because of a sex-tape which was exposed sometime back to the public by one of her lovers, a police-officer. He burnt himself to death, in front of a government office in London a few years later, when the British authorities declined to extend his visa. He maintained earlier that his life was in danger should he return to Nepal. Nowadays however, such scandals did not cause the suicide of an actress but only helped to push ahead her career, even in Nepal.

Then there was Dilip's ambition to pen a novel. He felt sorry for Nawin almost every time Dilip met him, for he took himself far too seriously as a writer. Writing anything less than a masterpiece would certainly disappoint him. Nawin just could not see that writing skills could also be used to make a living through a regular job, without compromising on one's ambition to write a book.

'Until we meet again,' Nawin thought, before he stood up and left the restaurant. He walked towards the bus stand, to catch a bus to his apartment. He was feeling some regret about speaking to Dilip harshly. After all, he was an old friend. But, fortunately, Dilip never appeared to take him seriously. He just liked to talk and then, with his mind preoccupied with his own thoughts, forgot entirely whatever they talked about.

Nawin thought, waiting for his bus, which was always overcrowded in the evening, that he and Dilip did the same to each other: accepted the other person talking while ignoring his thoughts. It was probably the basis of their friendship.

Some of Dilip's eccentricities might have been on account of his wife denying him sex often, as Dilip had once hinted. She was not happy that even after having a career in Kathmandu for nearly three decades, Dilip had still not managed to buy a home for his family. Since he was getting a chance to go to the USA now, perhaps he finally was making the right connections. Perhaps soon Dilip would buy a home and his marriage would improve.

But he was at least a decade late in catching up with the trend. There was already a crop of young editors educated at Harvard or New York University in Journalism, working at various media houses. They were drawing big amounts as salary and all the invisible perks, for making the right kind of noises and half-hearted protests, though most of the newspapers they worked for were hardly selling. It was no longer a mystery that they were sustained by businesses and the government, which were plundering the country. The people who were in favour of growth even on the face of dropping demand, were few but in a firm league with each other. Even a Maoist war against them had failed and its leaders had finally joined them.

'Poor, lazy Dilip! It is his pretension at morality which delays him, apart from his sexual adventures,' Nawin thought wryly. His friend was once again going to fail to make a kill.

Dilip had also informed him that his father-in-law, who had became a rich businessman of the town he belonged to and bought properties and businesses in Kathmandu to permanently shift, died in an accident on a highway recently. He used to visit his native town almost every month in his brand new Japan made SUV costing millions of rupees. To offer prayers at a temple there and to flaunt his vehicle, Dilip had added.

His father-in-law's friends back there still lived under the continuous threat of dying of snake-bites or water-borne diseases every monsoon season. Dying in an accident in a spectacular vehicle he was driving, was what his father-in-law might not have regretted much, Dilip had insisted.

His name and the name of the vehicle he was driving became a news for the next day's newspapers, occupying a few column-centimetres of them. It was a far too glamorous death than dying of diarrhoea, Dilip had added. The only more glamorous thing might have been to become a politician, which his father-in-law was aspiring to, and die in a crash while flying in a private jet, Dilip further had said. But he left nothing for his daughter, Dilip had complained.

Nawin felt more amused than sorry, on hearing it. The essential character of Dilip was largely intact, in spite of the dent time had made on it. He found his heart filling with kind feelings for Dilip.

Nawin smiled thinking how pretentious both of them might have sounded, discussing those serious matters in a cheap restaurant of a tourist area, like two rival politicians on a 'talk-show', who knew that it was, after all, a farce.

He recalled a royalist politician confessing in a newspaper interview that eating the Haluwa of raw bananas a little more than he should have, was the main deficiency of his character. People suspected him of amassing a fortune through corruption.

And there was a village-level Maoist leader talking on a FM channel. The Marxist jargons flew out of his mouth effortlessly, while he and his interviewer were trying hard to control the laughter about to erupt from them. Nawin wondered whether freedom made the people louder and more insecure. Before, they dithered to express any innocuous opinion, and dealt in generalities mostly. Now they asserted even their eccentricities as normal.

The people described by Tony Hagen, a Swiss traveller who travelled widely into the country when it hardly had any roads, in his books (full of pictures) - people who were too shy to smile even when they were asked for a photograph, were fast disappearing. The people who wished each other or a stranger with a shy smile and a tilt of head, instead of any words, were to be found only in the remotest part of Nepal.

The city was being represented by people in the show business or politics, who used Botox to hide their age but betrayed stained dirty teeth, whenever they smiled. They rode the most expensive SUVs, which earlier only had blue number plates, crowding the narrow streets of Kathmandu; streets which were full of litter and carcass of street dogs run over by such vehicles, and wore Swiss watches besides many rings on their fingers with colourful stones: a charm to avoid misfortune.

Meeting most people, Nawin felt, made him regretful.

The Redemption

NAWIN occasionally went to see his step-mother Nisha, and his half-brother Dinesh. Into her late seventies, Nisha's days were spent taking care of Dinesh. At times, of late, she was very worried about Dinesh, as age had slowed her down. It took her several hours to do the cooking or washing. Dinesh remained as he had always been: in his thirties now, with the intelligence of a three-year old. He had little capacity for comprehensible speech, although he talked a lot.

The District Medical Officer had certified him as totally handicapped, enabling Dinesh to get an allowance from the government. Nisha currently drew Dev's pension, and Dinesh would continue to receive it after she passed on. But money was not enough to compensate what providence had denied him. Somehow, he forgot the training given to him by his father on cleaning himself. He now depended on his mother even for washing his body or brushing his teeth.

In spite of everything, his step-mother brought stability into Nawin's life, which seemed adrift after the early death of his mother. Nawin recalled that once, when he was very young, he burnt his palm by trying to play with hot ashes. He returned home crying in pain. But he found his mother devoid of any consoling words. It was a woman of the neighbourhood who wiped his tears and put his palm in curd, saying that it was a case of burns. For one in pain, kind words work as much as the treatment. He looked with tearful eyes at his mother, who impassively watched like an onlooker.

Nisha, in comparison, was always reassuring. Even after the birth of Dinesh, late-motherhood did not change the affection she gave him and Anil, though the care of Dinesh had remained her main pre-occupation. She dutifully cooked for everybody and cleaned. When his father kept on smoking and coughed badly during the night, she often asked him to give up smoking. She also took care of her husband when he was bed-ridden for a few days before he passed away.

At times there were quarrels over Dinesh. Everyone in the house had his own ideas about his care. Disability had made him the centre of attention for everyone not just within the family, but including the people who visited them.

A bitter young age for Nisha, blighted by miscarriages and still-births, must have been tragic for her. Dev was often away, for his duties in the Army. Then, after her abandonment by Dev, when he took a second wife, to father a child, it must have been a lonely time. She never talked about it.

Late-motherhood, giving birth to a mentally-challenged child, when she came back to live with Dev, must have been beyond grief. After the death of Dev, taking care of Dinesh alone was even more tragic. To have survived all this in a lifetime would make most people suffer from depression. But she was in a remarkably good physical and mental health. Probably worrying about Dinesh's fate after her death kept her going.

For Nawin, there were also memories of the time, though brief, before Dinesh was born. It was when Nisha tried to give Nawin and Anil motherly affection when they were very young and insecure. A younger woman, married for the first time, like the sister of his mother, might not have been capable of it, Nawin often thought.

Nisha's days began early. She prepared tea and food, then washed and cleaned all morning. In the afternoon she rested for a while, before she prepared the evening meal for herself and

Dinesh. Perhaps remaining busy in household activities kept her healthy. Nawin could not recall if she ever was seriously sick. She was very thin and ate very little. Now her back was bent a little and she used a stick to support herself when she went out to buy milk or other essentials.

After the evening meal, when she had already made a bed for Dinesh and put him to sleep, on a day she felt cheerful, she hummed the folk songs she might have learnt in her childhood, and smoked tobacco in a bidi, before she too went to bed. Those songs were not much heard otherwise. They were about the life of a girl after she is married to an obstinate man, or about the life of a young mother, who had to arrange her child's life alone, while her husband was away.

When he was young, Nawin one night found her smoking, when everyone else in the family had gone to bed. He quarrelled with her on it and asked her to stop smoking. He thought, apart from men, only women of lower castes smoked. Such interference in her life Nisha protested and remained bitter about, for many days afterwards.

Age made Nawin wiser. He no more objected to her smoking, or other personal matters.

Living on her own, all those years, after the death of Dev, she had learned to manage her finances well. Before, she did not understand the different denominations of money and was not able to read a watch. Nawin discovered that she had managed things so well for her and Dinesh that she always had some surplus cash, saved from the pension she drew from her bank account by putting her thumb mark on the withdrawal slip. She also felt the power of surplus cash, as poor-relations now came to her to ask for it, when they were in need.

That made it possible for her to manipulate the relations. She got small services from them, like buying cooking gas or other essentials, or paying the bills for electricity or water, in exchange for the loans they took from her (which she knew shall never be paid back.) Also, she liked them coming to her as she could talk to them about the problems she had while taking care of Dinesh and enquire from them about relations who could not come to her.

Last time when he visited them, Nisha took him to the office, along with Dinesh, where she received her old-age pension and Dinesh his disability allowance. They had to climb a steep mountain to catch the jeep to reach the office one hour's drive away. With her walking stick in one hand, the other holding Dinesh's arm, she climbed effortlessly leaving Nawin almost breathless, though he was carrying their luggage. City life seemed to have compromised his fitness.

Before they left it was early morning. First she had made a breakfast of leftovers for them. She washed Dinesh and brushed his teeth. She double-locked the doors of the house and then carefully kept the keys in her bag. Nawin was astounded with her organising skills at nearly eighty. In the demure clothes of a widow, a brown woollen shawl across her shoulders, she looked a symbol of physical and moral strength to Nawin, while she walked in the feeble morning sun of a winter day, ahead of him and Dinesh.

After the death of his father, Dinesh had gained an enormous amount of weight; unlike his father, Nisha was not able to take him for walks every day. There was another mentally challenged girl of the same age as Dinesh in the town. Nawin went to meet her parents whenever he went to visit his home lately, as he felt an empathy and a natural bonding with them. They expressed genuine concern for Dinesh, asked about his habits and compared them to their daughter's. It was quite unlike the routine words of sympathy other people expressed.

Recently, the father of that invalid girl died, at a young age of fifty-five. Her mother, on his next visit, to express his condolences, told Nawin that only a day before, she wanted her daughter to die. She said that if the daughter outlived her, like she had her father, she would face great trouble. She speculated that mentally challenged children mostly die around the age of thirty, and that it was unusual that her daughter and Dinesh were such burdensome exceptions.

Nawin consoled her as best as he could, aware that, after the death of her husband, she was more worried about her daughter. He asked her to take care of herself, as she would have to live longer, to look after her daughter.

His heart was filled with more pity, on the thought that, sex, which proves such a driving force in the lives of normal people like him, eluded his half-brother Dinesh and that hapless girl, who also menstruated regularly. They both were virgins past the age of thirty. That unreleased energy, so potent a symbol of life, must have transformed the psyches of Dinesh and that girl in some strange ways. Nawin wondered what could be the manifestation of it in their personalities.

Nawin often found Nisha saying similar things about her own death and that of Dinesh. It happened more often if he was visiting home during winter, as the cold weather made her weaker and more irritable. A few days with them made Nawin so emotionally tired, that he hastened to return to Kathmandu, to his job and family.

But in his heart there always lurked the hardship Nisha bore. Also was there an ever-present fear, for what would happen if and when Nisha died. The duty of looking after Dinesh, after Nisha, intimidated Nawin. So the future was as uncertain as ever. Visiting once in a while to see Dinesh and Nisha could only be a symbol of his kind feelings towards them. By no means was it the real help Nisha needed so obviously. Nawin knew this well. He wished something to transpire that would relieve him of the financial worries of maintaining his family in Kathmandu, and devote more of his time to live with Nisha and Dinesh. But it was at best a few years ahead, as his children needed a few more years of schooling before they became independent.

He often thought of taking them to Kathmandu, to live with his family. But he still did not have a house of his own and the limited space of his apartment appeared small to him to accommodate Nisha and Dinesh. Nisha also was reluctant. All her life she had lived with certain relatives around. She had always lived in her own house. She wondered how she could live in a room in a city, not seeing any relations ever. Now she also was economically independent and was not willing to lose this status.

So he visited them for about a week at a time, every year or two. There were times when he saw a challenged child or man being taken care of by the guardian, in the streets of Kathmandu. It always led Nawin to think of Dinesh and he found his heart filling with pity, though there were occasions when he felt hostile towards Dinesh, especially when he kept on with his incomprehensible speech. Nawin wondered why the faces of all these challenged children looked alike, as if they were siblings, never mind how far apart they were living.

ONCE, when he started his journey home the Maoist war in the countryside was at its peak. There was a curfew on the highways during the night and the buses had to stop at sunset, and wait for dawn. Buses and their passengers were routinely inspected at regular check points. Nawin watched when his bus was checked at an outpost after Narayangarh. Soldiers walked onto the bus, weapons ready. With the barrel of an automatic weapon, his finger ready on the trigger, a soldier pointed to a piece of luggage and asked to whom it belonged. An absence of an immediate claim to it by someone would make it suspect, along with the owner of it. Thankfully, someone claimed the bag. The soldier did not bother to look into it. Of the two bags someone else claimed, the soldier asked him to open the other instead of the one the passenger was opening for checking.

The bus had to stop often, at times, for another kind of checking. Passengers were asked to carry their luggage to a counter nearly half a kilometre away. Troops observed them while walking, looking for anyone with an injury. Injured Maoists were routinely arrested by the Army at check points. They were usually on the way to India, to receive medical help.

The soldiers also interrogated people they suspected, while checking the luggage. The suspects were often young men wearing cheap jeans, who looked shabby in their thick uncut hair and Mongoloid faces. Some of them had their handkerchiefs tied on their forehead.

On reaching Butwal at 10:00 pm, the journey was stopped until four the following morning, due to the curfew on the highway. Thankfully, there was a hotel next to the petrol pump where the bus was parked, and Nawin was able to hire a room and rest.

There was an Israeli tourist on the bus who smoked hashish whenever the bus stopped. He had already found a few friends among the passengers to share the smoke with. He showed them a picture of a girl, saying that it was his girlfriend, who was waiting for him in Kullu in India. His hashish-smoking friends declined to believe him. One of them said that she looked like a Nepali. To it he laughed heartily and complained that the hashish in Nepal was of poor quality compared to that found in Shimla or Kullu.

He said his friends came to India mostly to use drugs. He came to Nepal to celebrate a festival, during which all the Jews in the area are expected to assemble in Kathmandu. He showed Nawin a book in Hebrew he was reading. He read it for Nawin, moving his finger from right to left. It was just like Urdu, to Nawin's amazement. That group smoked hashish all night and talked, disturbing others who were trying to sleep.

That evening the radio brought the news that a bomb blast by Maoists had injured three dozen people, near the post-office at Sundhara in Kathmandu. A young Tibetan refugee was among the passengers on the bus. He was in his early-twenties perhaps, as his boyish-face betrayed, though he was overweight to look middle-aged. He was born in India, and had never been to Tibet, he told Nawin. He spoke fluently in Hindi and English and managed a few sentences in Nepali too. He was gregarious and cracked jokes popular in India.

But he was confused about what male and female genitals were called in Hindi, which made the people laugh even more at his jokes. He had attracted a different group of young fellow-passengers, who had their own jokes to tell him. In spite of his funny manner, he was anxious. Perhaps that was what made him talk continuously. He told the people that, when he came to Nepal last time, the bus was so packed with the people returning for Dipavali that in the bus ahead of his, at Chisapani check post, a few of the returning Nepalese migrant-labourers from India were found tied by ropes to the luggage, on the roof of the bus.

The army men made sure, before they let the bus pass, that those people were tied at their request, of their own accord, by the staff of the bus. They were tied because of the fear of falling, should they fall asleep on a cold autumn night. The Tibetan added that they still needed to walk for two days to reach home, from the bus-stop they would be dropped at, high in the hills, towards the border with China. He was amazed that some Nepalese people were still as poverty stricken as that.

The Tibetan had many stories to tell.

It was around two in the morning. People on the bus who had not hired a room to rest at the hotel, including the Tibetan, became restless and started to make a lot of noise. They wanted the driver to resume the journey. He was sleeping in the hotel. Finding no response from any of the bus-staff or the fellow-passengers in the hotel, they started to sing popular folk songs, while beating the seats in the bus. Soon they fell silent. The bus resumed the journey at 5:00 am only.

There was more checking by the Army and the armed police. At one place a crowd had gathered. They were looking at a body covered by a sheet, near the shed serving as a waiting place for the passengers. The corpse was that of a policeman returning on leave to his village.

It happened around a festival day mostly, when security personnel took leave for a day or two to be with their families. And the Maoists just waited for them to come home.

The Maoists heard about him. They came and stabbed him to death, after torturing him to collect the information about the enemy.

Nobody touched his body, for fear of the Maoists. It was expected that security officials would come to provide protection to cremate the body of that hapless policeman.

By then, families of men serving in the security forces were being threatened by the local Maoists, to ask them to resign. Many ran away to India, deserting the army, while some joined the Maoists along with their weapons.

A little farther along the journey they again stopped. The road was blocked this time. Maoists had cut a few trees with their branches intact from the thick jungle covering both sides of the highway and dragged them to the road. Sunlight had started to illuminate the green hills in the north a little distance away. It was a beautiful autumn morning. People expected to celebrate the festivals and holidays in the days ahead though travelling on those highways was not easy. The night buses and other vehicles were approaching, making the waiting crowd of held-up passengers bigger with each fresh arrival.

Getting out of their vehicles, some passengers made a crowd a little distance away from the blockage. Nobody went near the trees blocking the road, fearing the explosives which may go off. A helicopter appeared after a few hours, from the opposite side, from behind the forests. The base-station of armed-police was not far. It hovered for a while and then returned. The passengers began gossiping about what would happen next. Some of them exchanged their experiences when they were earlier held-up like this, in different areas of the country.

The Maoist war was about a decade old. It seemed to have touched the life of almost every one travelling, in the roads covered by forests and the hills not too far away. The geographical conditions were ideal for a protracted guerrilla war.

In a recent incident, the younger brother of a friend of Nawin was killed. He was travelling from Biratnagar to Rajbiraj in the east of the country. Working for a pharmaceutical company, he had to call upon the doctors. His bus was caught in a cross-fire in the early morning on the highway. A single bullet pierced his lung on the right side. He died before help arrived. He was just twenty-two, and was not married yet.

Nawin went with his friend to the office of Home Ministry at Singhdurbar, a few months later. It was to receive the payment of one lakh rupees, his friend got as compensation. It was mentioned in the papers that his friend signed that his brother was killed by a bullet from the Maoist side. Mentioning that it was a bullet from the security forces might not only have entailed more enquiries but also a bigger compensation from the government.

Passengers began discussing the huge casualties the Maoists were receiving recently. The Army, under the leadership of the new king, was on an offensive. Many Maoist ambushes of outposts ended in disaster. The rebels ran away carrying their wounded or dead comrades. Later, security forces discovered hastily dug common graves; each with nearly a dozen bodies piled one upon another. The stories with pictures were spilled by newspapers in Kathmandu. It seemed as if the tide was slowly turning, and the Maoists were on the run, finally.

There were rumours that fighters seriously wounded but not dead were also buried, as the retreating guerrillas were not able to carry them. Injured rebels could leak the intelligence, if found alive. Yet in some places the Maoists were winning, killing all the security personnel at an outpost, who had surrendered, and taking away their weapons.

The Maoists now had several M16 rifles, as shown in the newspaper pictures by the journalists who went deeper into the hinterland to talk with them, risking the wrath of the state and the hostility of the security forces. Even the foreign journalists had an easy access to the rebels. The human rights' activists had done a great job in securing the basic rights of people even while a very dirty civil war was in progress.

The rebels had AK 47 rifles too, which were not used by any of the security forces in Nepal. They were getting weapons from other sources too, from outside the country.

The taking over of power by the king had made the war more open. Day-to-day politics, which was creating confusion among the security forces, on how to deal with the situation, which was claiming more lives of their ranks, was there no more, after the king took over. This situation strangely drifted the democratic political parties towards the Maoists, and against the king.

An hour after the helicopter left, a truck full of Army men arrived. After making sure that there were no hidden explosives, they carefully removed the trees from the road. The buses moved ahead, and stopped an hour's drive later. The passengers disembarked. Some of them started brushing their teeth, before they had the breakfast at the eating places under the roof of dried grass, over walls of mud and wood.

Nawin felt sceptical about the people, who were getting on with their daily activities so normally, after a night's journey full of so many uncertainties and unpleasant surprises (apart from being a sleepless one). They gobbled up boiled eggs, beans and sel rotis.

The Israeli tourist had a little juice and was smoking again his hashish cigarettes. Nawin had his black tea. The tourist told Nawin that he had recently completed his mandatory military service and was on holiday. He was bitter when he talked about his experience in the Army. He was just a few years past twenty, and was tall and slim. A brown beard covered his handsome face, under the thick hair on his head. He wished that the war in Nepal would end soon.

As soon as they reached the next base of the Army, a few hours' drive further, half of the passengers left the bus. They were Army men returning to duty from holidays. Nawin was surprised that no one doubted their identity, including the security people checking the bus so often. Travelling with so many security personnel in a vehicle was full of risk for the civilians, as Maoists had recently blown-up one such bus in Chitwan. About two dozen civilians were killed, apart from a few of the security personnel in the bus. Maoists had warned the civilians to avoid travelling with security people in public transport vehicles. But civilian vehicles were the safest transport for the security people, as Maoists had blown off many of their vehicles on different highways, at times killing a high ranking official as well.

By afternoon they approached the border with India. The Israeli tourist was the only other person from his bus, going to India. Nawin heard the tourist complain that the officials at immigration desk would pester him for *baksis* or tips, both in India and Nepal, though he had a valid visa. Nawin deliberately allowed him to go a little ahead.

He was worried that the tourist still had drugs on him. He did not want to be seen as his friend or companion. If the drugs were discovered by officials of either India or Nepal, he too could land in serious trouble. While the tourist was undergoing the formalities at the immigration office, with his back to him, Nawin hastily crossed the border.

That evening he rested at a comfortable hotel, at Tanakpur, just near the railway station, finally enjoying a shower and the delicious food it served.

LAST time when he went home, he did not cross the border to rest at Tanakpur. Instead he went north from Attaria in a comfortable Japanese minibus. In the south of Attaria was Dhangadi. The highway reaching his home was in an excellent condition. It was two-lanes broad throughout, and had been created by cutting through the mighty rocks of the mountains. Climbing ever higher, they were about to reach the ancient town of Dadeldhura when the bus broke down, nearly twenty kilometres away.

It needed a major repair, the driver discovered. He sent his helper on another bus passing by, to call another bus of his company, to shift his passengers into that. It entailed a wait of few hours. He rejected the request of the passengers to return their money for the remaining journey, who wanted to catch one of the passing buses. Returning money would have been a loss to the bus driver.

Nawin tuned into the BBC world service on a FM radio channel, on his mobile phone. A black man was being interviewed. He was going to the USA from London, to take part in the inaugural ceremony of the newly elected President Obama.

Dadeldhura, situated on a high spot, open on two sides, was the coldest place Nawin had been to for some time, though it was still autumn. The strong cold-wind made him shiver. It blew continuously, making the sun ineffective. The land was sparsely populated and thick jungles covered most of the landscape next to the town. The valley on the other side had crops in strips of land, but no settlement. He had crossed a few villages before, the road bisecting them. On either side were trees full of big, yellow oranges.

It was the first time Nawin had taken this route. He wondered how the road next to their houses had affected the lives of the villagers, who earlier walked for several days before they rode a bus. By now the king had been dethroned and Nepal had become a republic. One was reminded of it often by the bank notes not having the picture anymore, rather than anything else. The picture of Mount Everest had replaced it. If a country was about its people, none of them looked good enough to appear on the Nepalese bank notes.

Maoists, after sweeping the elections, were leading the coalition government ruling the country. King Gyanendra accepted the verdict of the people and retired to the bungalow the government gave him to live in the forest of Nagarjuna, in the hills west of Kathmandu. But he was hopeful of returning to the Narayanhiti Royal Palace he had vacated, as the constitution in making was becoming more controversial with each passing day. Various ethnic groups were demanding a state within a state, threatening the country to disintegrate into several parts. The political violence was claiming more lives than during the Maoist war.

At the town of Dadeldhura was the fort of Amargadhi, named after the warrior Amar Thapa, who led the Nepalese army to defeat the British-Indian army, which occupied ever-deeper into the territories in South Asia, a long time back. The fort was in the control of the Army, and Nawin's efforts to have a closer look did not materialise. He recalled that there was a statue of Amar Thapa in Almora also, in India, where he went to school for a few years.

After Dadeldhura, he caught a jeep going to Baitadi. The traffic thinned even more and the landscape became emptier of settlements. On the far right, there were peaks of the mighty

He found Nisha calmly sitting near Dinesh at home. In her fingers ran a thread of cotton she was twisting out of the dollop she held in another hand. The thread was consolidated with the movement of her fingers before it was broken away from the dollop. Then another thread would appear in her hands, when she picked one more tiny thread from the dollop and started twisting again. These threads she would burn in oil in the evening, when she would offer her prayers to the deities in their home.

Finding both of them content and healthy, Nawin felt immensely happy.

It was a picture he had in his mind always, when he was away from them. He had made the tiresome journey, just to see them and feel redeemed. His hand inadvertently touched the old, wrinkled and toothless face of his step-mother. He held her chin in his palm for a moment, with tears in his eyes. He remembered it was what she did to him when he was very young, after his mother had died.

Acknowledgements

I thank Victor Schwartzman, a well-known Canadian poet, for helping me prepare the manuscript of this novel.